The Library and the Forest

Twice

Dear Atinuke
Thank you for all you are —

Anthony Buckley

Love & prayers
Anthony

Published by New Generation Publishing in 2024

Copyright © Anthony Buckley 2024

First Edition

The author asserts the moral right under the Copyright, Designs and Patents Act 1988 to be identified as the author of this work.

All Rights reserved. No part of this publication may be reproduced, stored in a retrieval system or transmitted, in any form or by any means without the prior consent of the author, nor be otherwise circulated in any form of binding or cover other than that which it is published and without a similar condition being imposed on the subsequent purchaser.

ISBN   978-1-83563-195-9

www.newgeneration-publishing.com

New Generation Publishing

For Lydia and Richard

Further thanks to all who have kindly encouraged, including the forensic and challenging readers: Hannah, Miranda, Myriam and Steph; the remaining mistakes are mine, especially the commas.

And to M, F, R, K, for patience, and firm thoughts about the title.

Contents

Chapter 1: The Library and the Invitation 1

Chapter 2; The Find in the River 5

Chapter 3: The Regathering Begins......................... 11

Chapter 4: Edward Makes a Choice 15

Chapter 5: The Circle Widens 23

Chapter 6: A Trap and the Dragon 26

Chapter 7: The Confrontation................................... 34

Chapter 8: Agnes Tells Her Story............................. 44

Chapter 9: An Unexpected Task............................... 52

Chapter 10: The Wisdom of the Hermit 58

Chapter 11: The Grailstand is Sought...................... 67

Chapter 12: Restoration 72

Chapter 13: The Call of the Sea................................ 78

Chapter 14: The Battle Becomes Clearer 80

Chapter 15: Playing the Game Well 85

Chapter 16: Violence and Rescue............................. 93

Chapter 17: Glimpses of the View............................ 98

Chapter 18: Return to St George's........................ 102

Chapter 1: The Library and the Invitation

There was a rope across the bottom of the stairs. Hanging crookedly from the rope was a sign that simply said: 'No Entry'.

It was a bright spring morning and Mark Lind was making one of his occasional returns to the local library where an advertisement many years earlier had set him in a new direction: working in a school, joining a circle of friends, and playing a role in a bigger drama than he could have previously imagined. When he was in the library, he (slightly self-consciously) liked to sit at the same table on the first floor, if it was free. And today his way was barred.

He looked around, began to walk to a desk he thought was empty at the other end of the library. *It may not be the same desk, but at least it is the same building,* he thought, and then caught sight of a notice on the wall.

Can you tell stories? Come and join us on Monday afternoons and entertain a small group of children after school!

Mark smiled, slightly wistfully. Could he even still tell stories? After all these years? And he had never really sought to 'entertain'. He wondered whose attention might be caught. It was exciting to think of someone in the next generation, much more entertaining and vibrant than he could be, perhaps good at dressing up, dramatically striding across the floor, putting on different voices, enthusing the audience. He could imagine such a person responding to the notice, and then – who knows what might happen?

He had paused for a moment. Stirring himself he looked on, but someone else now sat at the empty desk. He realised there was no room for him and he headed back towards the entrance, regretting his silliness that morning at wanting to come back to the library at all. The lady at the reception table hurried over and intercepted him: "I saw you looking at the notice. Are you interested? Please say yes. It is only three children from the school across town. Two teachers bring them. We look after them for half an hour."

Mark smiled. "You mean that notice? I'm sure there will be someone better." He paused. "Why do the children come here? Why don't they go straight home?"

"I don't know all the details; I get the impression things are complicated. A neutral space (not quite a school, not quite home) was requested. And the school wanted it to be a learning space, and so the library was suggested."

"Which school are they from?"

"St George's, which happens to be my old school," said the receptionist.

Mark said thoughtfully and cautiously, "I know of St George's." And then, with a slight question in his voice, "It is good of the school or council to be funding this." Another pause: "There really will be better, younger, more entertaining, people than me; I hope you find someone soon." He laid an unnecessary, somewhat defensive, stress on the 'entertaining', and then felt rather guilty. The library was only trying to do its best.

The lady flushed and looked slightly awkward. She said hesitantly, "It is being funded by the school. But then someone came in, looked at the notice, and seemed to know something was happening, and he said that if an older, hesitant, gentleman came in, likely to be wearing a not-very-new tweed jacket, and saw the notice, then the gentleman might initially say no but may end up saying yes. He even said that the person may not charge a fee."

She looked at Mark, up and down, "Is that you?"

I think I recognise the voice. What do we really mean when we speak of time standing still? Is it the realisation that a larger narrative is happening, too large to be contained within the counting of seconds? Is it the sense of being quieted into pausing, because something so significant is unfolding before our eyes? When we talk about being 'taken aback', is that as much about the clock-hand being held back as about us physically being startled backwards?

Mark realised he had become a little rambling in his thoughts; the lady was looking at him, fidgeting even more: "I probably made a mistake, perhaps it is not right for you after all. Thank you so much."

"It may be right," Mark replied, softly. "What sort of stories are needed?"

The lady relaxed slightly (had she got the right jacket but the wrong person, or was the right person going to be slightly odd, and she had been right?) "Oh, to be honest, anything with good role models would help, that is what the school says they need. Anything with hope. Courage would be good, too." She paused. "Life is not always easy, is it?"

Mark nodded, non-committedly, and then asked: "Who is the Headteacher of the school these days?"

Her voice became neutral. "Mrs Hutchinson. I have not met her. When I was there it was Mr Edge."

Mark noticed the change of tone and decided not to pursue that, but rather to bring the conversation back. "I think it might indeed be me that the person had in mind." He paused and then said quietly, "And he was right, there will be no charge. When do we start?"

The receptionist smiled broadly. "Next Monday, if you are free? And thank you… thank you so much."

"One last thing," asked Mark. "Why are the stairs closed today?"

"No one goes up there much anymore. It is just easier to close it off."

Chapter 2; The Find in the River

The following Monday afternoon Mark looked at the three children, aged about eleven or twelve, sitting or lying on large cushions. Their teachers sat on chairs behind them. The lady smiled encouragingly from behind the reception desk. Mark welcomed the pupils, found out that their names were Trudy, Sarah and Jason, and that their teachers were Miss Smith and Mr Cook. And then he began.

***

Edward had been in the forest most of the morning and was on his way home. He could see the wisps of smoke swirling up behind the cottage. This was an encouraging sign, something was cooking; it must be nearly lunch.

He liked the forest. He was twelve years old and understood that it provided so much for the village: wood, fuel, tools, weapons. He knew it was always changing, living and dying, breathing and beginning. And it lived the seasons. A frosty path was as fresh and exciting as a summer morning. Fallen leaves as much as spring blossom.

Of course he had not really been *in* the forest that morning, just the part of it near the path. There was always more than enough to explore there, even though he knew it very well. He seldom went further in. The forest spread far, and the mystery of it, and one or two glances or words that adults had let slip, made him think it was not safe to venture too deep.

He was right about the cooking. His mother had lit the fire and the soup in the pot was beginning to bubble. Lunch would not be far away. She looked round and smiled.

"Did you see anything?"

"No animals, except a rabbit. I think the badger sett is growing. And that old dead tree I told you about, it is going to come down soon. But still probably strong enough for me to climb."

He said the last sentence to see if he could stir up the suddenly watchful look in his mother's eyes. He was right, he could. He smiled.

"Don't worry. I am careful."

She sighed with false exaggeration, smiled in return, nodded, and looked back at the pot. "I'll finish this while you get the table ready." Edward went inside. Getting the table ready meant unwrapping the bread from its cloth, putting it on the table, and finding two spoons.

"The monastery this afternoon?" his mother asked. It was a statement as much as a question. She had wanted Edward to be able to read and learn and had arranged with Prior John that one of the Monks would teach him an hour a day. The Prior hoped to set up a school one day, but, until that could be organised, he was pleased to offer help to anyone who wished to learn.

Edward enjoyed the lessons. He liked the sense of connection with the past. As his fingers traced the letters and as he tried to say the words, he felt himself part of something much older and wider. Rather like being in the forest.

He was learning to read Latin, and occasionally Brother James would tell him stories about Athens, Rome and Jerusalem. *These great cities,* Edward would think, with a thrill: *These great adventures. And I am reading what others have read, I am reading what someone long ago wrote. Someone who knew the streets and the buildings, the smells and the noises.* And he would imagine the processions and the chariots, the great stones and the pillars, the arches and the voices.

The lesson that afternoon went well. Brother James was cheerful, as he usually was. Very occasionally he was downcast and Edward would ask why. The monk might mention an illness in the infirmary, or fear for the village if a sudden storm meant that the harvest might be poor and cottages damaged, or would quietly shake his head and Edward knew not to press further. But today Brother James was in good spirits, the learning was cheerful.

The journey home from the monastery could be straight back along the path or a longer walk by the river. (Brother James had told Edward that monks liked to place their monasteries close to water so people and floors could be kept clean). It was an autumn day and the light was lessening, but there was still enough warmth in the air and there was no hurry.

Edward decided to walk by the river. He went steadily and slowly, enjoying sights and sounds and breezes. Glancing this way and that he noticed something floating in the river, catching the glint of the late afternoon sun. Edward knew that the river was shallow here and three strides took him near enough to reach out and hold it. He clambered back on the bank, wondering if his clothes would dry before he got home, and looked carefully at what he had found. He had been fortunate to see the glint. The sun must have glanced it at just the right moment; only a small part of it was shiny, the rest was blackened. It was like a bracelet, but thick and heavy, and slightly bigger than usual.

When he arrived home his mother decided that the clothes could be draped and dried over the table, so all was well.

She had learned that whatever Edward had been doing, whatever state he was in, he needed to know he was welcomed home. And that meant being calm and smiling. If questions needed to be asked, they could come later.

Edward found some clothes of his father who had died some years before. They were still too big for him but were more than enough for moments like this. As time went by, the clothes grew slightly closer to a fit, but there was a year or two to go yet.

Edward showed her his find. She turned it over and tried it on her wrist. "It seems big for a bracelet, and too heavy," she said.

"That's what I thought. I think there are letters on it, but I can only make out I, C, and then P," said Edward. "Shall I take it to Brother James tomorrow?"

"That is a good idea. Now, tell me what you learned about today."

They talked for a little while and then it was time for bed.

The next morning he went back to the monastery and took the bracelet (he could think of no other word – perhaps it was the bracelet of a giant) with him.

Brother James looked at it carefully and then said, "May I take it and show it to Prior John?"

Edward nodded and sat back, looking out from the cloister into the calm square of grass.

It was some time before the monk came back, and Prior John, whom Edward had only met once, was with him. Edward stood up, Prior John gestured him to sit and sat across the cloister from him.

"Edward, thank you for bringing this to show us. Brother James tells me you saw the letters I, C, space, then P?"

Edward said. "I thought it might be 'Hic' something."

"I agree about the letters. You are a good pupil, you look keenly and think well. You are very likely to be right on the 'Hic'. We will all agree that the P is more difficult but there is one clear possibility."

Edward looked across to where Brother James was sitting; there was no sign or response, but he wondered if he was looking more watchful, thoughtful, than usual. *There is something going through his mind*, Edward wondered to himself.

"Brother James is a wise and careful scholar," continued Prior John, who had noticed the glance and the questioning eyes. "And he wondered if this may indeed be important, so he brought it to me. Edward, this is not a bracelet. It is a holder, a stand, for something. In practical terms it was unnecessary; what it would surround would be able to stand firm and true on its own, but it is a sign of the keeper's honouring of what was entrusted to him or her. Unnecessary perhaps, but dignified and beautiful."

"What would it have held?" asked Edward.

"The words could have been *Hic Ponitur*." Prior John raised an eye in question, but Edward shook his head, his Latin could not reach it. The Prior continued "It means *Here it is placed.*"

"What would the 'it' have been?" asked Edward.

"Edward, this might have held a special goblet or a chalice. I have only heard of one like it before."

"And what was that one?"

"That one was made to hold the Holy Grail; it was called the Grailstand."

Edward's eyes grew large and there was silence. The cloisters, strong and permanent in stone and light, suddenly seemed insubstantial and fleeting. He tried to say something but there was nothing he felt he could say.

Prior John smiled. "But perhaps there were others that I have not heard about. Perhaps this is not the Grailstand."

Edward breathed slowly, a couple of times, and tried to sound calm: "Whatever it is, or held, it looked scorched to me. How would it have been burnt?"

Brother James spoke, "Edward, the river flows from deep within the forest."

He glanced across, Prior John nodded and leaned forward. "Edward, how much do you know about dragons?"

"Nothing."

***

Trudy, Sarah, and Jason, sitting on the cushions, waited, but Mark looked at the clock on the wall and said, "We should stop there for today; it is time to go. Thank you for listening so well. See you next week?"

Jason put up his hand: "But *everyone* knows about dragons."

Mark smiled. "More next week."

Chapter 3: The Regathering Begins

When the children were gone, led away by Miss Smith and Mr Cook, Mark stood up. He pushed his chair neatly back against the wall and walked to the end of the bookshelf that partially screened the corner so it could be a place set aside for storytelling. He happened to glance back to his right and saw someone sitting at the far end, hidden from view when he had been speaking to the children.

"A story well-told, Mr Lind," the person said, softly.

Mark looked more carefully. Could it be?

"Jane!" He said, with much excitement but as quietly as he could.

"Let's go outside," Jane whispered back. "Libraries are not good places for raucous reunions." She got up and they left, Mark thanking the lady at the desk as they went.

On the pavement, Mark asked, "Were you listening?"

"Of course," said Jane, "As I did in your interview; what is it, twenty-five years ago now?" She paused, "I was asked to be here because the rumour reached me that Sir Richard was ready to ride out one more time."

"And who, dear Jane, may have started that rumour?"

"We both know the source of good rumours. Come on my old friend, I have been asked to take you to him now." She grabbed his arm and looked at her watch. "We are meeting them in the park, we should be going."

The warmth of the April afternoon was fading and the shadows beginning to lengthen. In the park there was a small garden especially cultivated, set aside with low walls, with winding paths, statues, flowers and trees. Jane led the way, followed one of the paths, and they ended up at a small, circular, stone folly. There was a stone bench running around the inside; sitting in the middle, facing the entrance and looking down across the garden and then across the park itself, was Rex English. Next to him sat Jenny Loss.

Mr English (former Headmaster of St George's) and Jenny Loss (former teacher) opened their hands in greeting to them. Jane and Mark took their places on the bench.

"You are welcome," Mr English said. "As always and ever."

"How was the story?" asked Jenny Loss.

"What I liked," said Jane, "was that Mr Lind did his best." And the four of them smiled.

"That is always enough," said Mr English. "And I ask for no more."

"Why the old tweed jacket?" said Mark. "Could there not have been a more noble or heroic sign?"

"It is part of you; why give you a sign that is not? If Lancelot had been called to the task, then the sign might have been the glint of a noble sword beneath a cloak. But the library would have been more likely to call the police than offer him a job. Make do with the faded jacket, dear Mark. It is not a bad symbol."

"It has been a long time," said Mark.

Mr English paused. "Were you beginning to forget that you were Merlin? Such things are possible; people do forget their callings, often not intentionally."

"I don't think I had forgotten, but it seemed more in the past than the present."

"A calling may be quiet for one season, or expressed differently in another, but it is still there. It is not withdrawn."

"Mr English," said Jane, with a slight bow and the usual twinkle in her eyes, "I have come to report that the rumour is correct that Sir Richard is ready to ride out again."

Mark said, "And why, dear Jane, should he be identified with me?"

"Because he was in the first story you told."

"Perhaps he was someone I wanted to tell a story about, or even wanted to be like, but that is not the same thing as saying it is me."

"It may be quite close."

Mark paused, and the pause was long, and the others held the silence. Eventually he said, "Perhaps Sir Richard is always ready with the right nudge. But I don't know where or why I am riding."

Rex English said, with a gentle authority that was making a statement, not asking a question: "Many great quests have been undertaken by those who knew not the why or the how."

Mark looked around the circle. The physical effects of the years varied, but there was little change in who they were: "Are you still in touch with the others?"

"From time to time," answered Mr English. "If they knew you were here, they would send warm greetings."

"Mr Moore?"

"Retired from St George's some years ago, he has not been in touch. I do not know if he would send greetings." And a sadness passed over his face.

Into the silence came Jenny's voice: "We should be grateful that there are some libraries still open, Mark, the stories continue. It is very good to see you again."

"Until I know what is going on, I guess I keep telling the story?" Mark asked.

"I rather think you should." said Mr English.

Chapter 4: Edward Makes a Choice

Next Monday. Mark was in the library. The lady at the desk had greeted him warmly, as if he was now an old friend. The three children and teachers were already there.

***

Prior John leaned forward. "Edward, how much do you know about dragons?"

"Nothing."

"Not many people know very much about them these days. Some do, but not everyone."

Mark looked at Jason and gave a quick smile; Jason's eyes lit up and he gave a broad smile in return.

"Let me try and explain. Many years ago there were several in this land. They roamed where they wished, eating what they could find, devouring with fire when roused. As people spread further and made stronger weapons, the number of dragons grew less. They became more secretive, making their homes in deep caves. Occasionally stories would be told of a sheep lost from a flock, or a calf from a herd, and villagers would wonder if a dragon was nearby, but no one has seen one for a long time. Some wonder if there are any left.

"There is an old rumour that far in the forest, where the darkness and magic are deepest, there may still be one of the old dragons. A dragon would be able to sense the goodness in the Grailstand (if that is what it is) and would try to destroy it. Hence the burn marks. Or perhaps the dragon attacked the person who was carrying the Grailstand at the time."

After some moments, Edward said. "If the Grailstand was there, might the Grail be?"

"No," said Prior John. "A long time ago it went elsewhere." And Edward sensed he would not say more.

Prior John looked at the floor and marked the lengthening shadows: "I see the hours have passed; I think that is enough for today."

Edward felt he knew what he should be asking, although he was hesitant to do so. "Is there something you want me to do?"

"Come back tomorrow," said Prior John, "and I will suggest, and you can decide. It is time now to go home."

When he was home, and supper (soup) was cleared away, Edward talked it over with his mother. He spent a restless evening. He knew deep down that he was likely to say 'yes' to whatever he might be asked to do, and he did not know if that would be a safe thing to do. He cared for his mother very much and was beginning to realise that he mattered in the welfare of their home.

The next day he was back in his familiar seat in the cloister. "In times to come," said Prior John. "There will be an age when stories will be written to say that dragons are misunderstood, that they, whatever the appearance, are really rather friendly. I need to tell you that they are not. One of my callings as Prior is to remind people that dragons are what they are."

He paused, and then said, "We would like to know about this dragon, whether indeed it is there at all. Dragons are dangerous, beyond easily reckoning. And as time goes by they become stronger and larger. They do not weaken by being left alone."

Edward shuffled slightly.

Prior John paused, and then continued: "The three of us, and Abbess Francesca in the monastery across the valley whom I talked to this morning, are the only ones who know about the scorched Grailstand. We do not wish too many to know that there may be a dragon in the forest, until we know what we are going to do. Worry spreads fast."

Edward looked up, a question in his eyes.

"I consulted the Abbess because her wisdom is beyond mine," replied the Prior. "She is wise and learned in herself, and her family is from across the water. She has a broad perspective, as well as years of study."

Edward knew it was the time to ask again the question from yesterday.

"What do you want me to do?"

"Go into the forest, carefully, very carefully," the prior said calmly. "And see what happens. But go home first, there is someone there to meet you."

The sun was ebbing in the cloisters, and Edward felt that all the comfort and familiarity of the stone and the grass were fading, too.

He walked home thoughtfully. Prior John had spoken but Edward knew that it was his choice to make. The edges of the forest had always been enough for him, and now he was being introduced to a world of relics and dragons, of mystery and danger.

He was turning all this over in his mind and was not looking ahead as he usually would. And so, when nearing home, he did not see the figure sitting on the spare stool, talking to his mother outside the cottage, until he was almost there.

His mother smiled and said, "Edward, this is Abbess Francesca. Fetch your stool and join us."

Once he had done so, the Abbess looked kindly at him. "What are you thinking?"

Edward sensed that she knew what conversations had happened, and so he simply said: "I am not sure that I want to go. And I do not know why it has to be me."

"You do not have to go, and it does not have to be you. But you know the forest, or some of it. And you found the Grailstand. That gives you the right to be asked. You might get further, be less noticeable, than a band of adults. You like the forest, and the forest usually treats well those who like it."

"I am a child." Edward looked at his mother.

"Children are not exempt from quests," said Francesca, gently.

Edward shrugged his shoulders, slightly helplessly.

"I cannot fight a dragon."

"Prior John and I both feel that it might be right for you, having found the Grailstand, to look further. I have come here today to assure your mother and you that I think you will be safe. That much I can say."

Edward looked at his mother, who nodded.

"And," continued the Abbess, "I am sending a young member of my order, Agnes, to go with you."

"If I am to go, I am happy going alone. I am used to being by myself."

"Sometimes it is right to travel together," Francesca said, slightly more firmly. "Edward, when we are called to a quest, we are part of a larger fellowship, and each must play their part. In this instance, mine is to guide, and my guidance is for Agnes to join you."

Edward had the feeling that this was more command than guidance. He knew he was not a little boy, but wished he could be again. He felt too young to do what he was being called to do, and too old to be what he wanted still to be. And so he said, not very cheerfully or graciously, "I will go, and I will go with Agnes."

"I will send a message to Prior John with that news and will bring Agnes here tomorrow morning. Thank you for making your choice." She smiled, reached out and took his hand. "I think you have chosen wisely, and I honour your courage."

Edward nodded. He did not feel much better, but he was grateful.

The next morning Agnes came to the cottage with Abbess Francesca. She was a little older than Edward. The children sat silently as the adults talked further for a few minutes; they then said goodbye and walked down the path and into the forest. They still did not say very much. Although the silence was slightly awkward Edward was grateful for it; he was not very good at conversation, unless it was *about* something.

Agnes was thoughtful. She trusted Abbess Francesca, who had told her about the Grailstand and Edward. But when she arrived at the cottage there had been a sudden fear that the adults – the Abbess and the Prior – were getting this wrong, were making a mistake. She could not quite lose the fear. What might happen to her, and this boy Edward? She was an orphan and lived in Abbess Francesca's monastery. She had no family, but she was part of things there. It was her home, and it all seemed a long way away.

They passed through the part of the forest that Edward knew best, but then continued inwards. Edward had expected it to become more overgrown and darker, more difficult to penetrate, but it was the opposite. The trees were more spaced apart, the sun easily reached the forest floor. The walking felt easier, and slightly less interesting.

But Edward felt exposed. There were fewer hiding places. He suddenly wondered if he were being watched, and he kept looking from side to side, and behind.

"It feels strange," nodded Agnes. "And silent." She looked up into the trees. "Where are the birds? I can hear nothing."

The children stopped, without quite knowing why. And then, ahead of them, they saw a figure moving toward them.

"I still don't really know why we are here," said Edward, trying hard not to let the desperation show.

Agnes answered, "I don't think we would have been sent if this was not right for us." But there was a slight shake in her voice. "I hope that is true."

Edward did not look at her. And he shrugged a slightly miserable shrug.

The figure was walking quickly. Strangely, given the openness of this part of the forest, Agnes and Edward felt trapped. There seemed no point in running. They instinctively reached out, held hands, and waited.

The figure drew nearer. They saw it was a man (they both had been secretly scared that it might not be a person at all). He was wearing a long cloak and his hood was flung back. He stopped, about ten yards away.

"What are your names?"

"I am Agnes, and this is Edward."

"You are honoured to be named after martyrs. Have you their truth and courage?"

It was neither a question they were expecting nor wanted.

"What is *your* name?" said Agnes.

"Mine can wait."

"That's unfair," blurted out Edward.

The man came closer. And he smiled.

***

Mark stopped. "We will leave it there for this week."

"What happened next?" asked Trudy. "What sort of smile?"

"More next week."

"No, I need to know. What sort of smile?"

Mark glanced over the children's heads and saw Mr Cook and Miss Smith watching intently, watching Trudy, watching him. He knew he had to say something. "I cannot give too much away, but I think I can say, it was a nice smile."

"There are smiles and smiles, even when they seem nice," said Trudy.

"It was a nice smile, and a true one," said Mark, and he sensed the challenge and tension melting. "Let's go now, see you next week."

"Why didn't they run?" asked Sarah.

"They were confused and scared, and perhaps for some of us it is not always easy to do the obvious thing? But the story may end well."

The children did not respond. Mr Cook said, "Well, it really is time we went now."

Chapter 5: The Circle Widens

Mark made his way from the library to the folly in the park; there was no one there and he sat and reflected on the afternoon. He thought about Trudy and Sarah's reaction. *Perhaps we are always treading on sensitive ground, and it is not for us to know, but if there is goodwill underneath it, perhaps not too much harm will be done.* He was glad he had sacrificed a suspenseful climax to ensure that reassurance had been given. *You can't always be wanting to make an impact,* he smiled to himself. *Sometimes you just need to be kind.*

He heard footsteps on the path and Jane came in, followed by someone Mark had not seen for many years.

"Hello, Mark," she said, and held out both hands to him.

Mark took the offered hands. "Hello, Emma," he replied. "I did wonder if I might be seeing you before too long."

But before he could say more, he realised that Jenny Loss was behind Emma and so they all shuffled in a little (the folly was not large) and sat down. Mark was just about to speak when Jenny raised her hand: "There are steps on the path. I think someone else is joining us."

A figure was framed in the doorway. It was the lady from the reception desk at the library.

"I followed you," she said quickly, looking at Mark. "And then I was nervous and waited, and then saw the others come in. I don't know them. I hope you don't mind. And this must feel very strange and odd to you that I am here."

"No more than you knowing to look out for someone in an old tweed jacket," said Mark. "You are very welcome. This is Jane, whom you may remember from the library a couple of weeks ago. And this is Emma and Jenny, we are old friends."

"It is very nice to meet you all, but I don't want to interrupt. I'll try another time."

"Perhaps we were meant to be here this afternoon to listen to you," said Jenny. "Say what you need to say."

The lady nodded and gulped. "You see, you see, my name is Agnes. And I don't know many Agneses, or read stories with Agneses in them. And your story includes one." Her words all came out in a rush. "I am not sure what to think. Was all this *meant* to happen? Someone coming dressed like you, just like that person said he would be. And then the story with my name in it? I don't know whether to feel trapped or excited."

"Feeling excited is usually a more positive and helpful response," said Jenny, with a smile. "Stay with that rather than feeling trapped. I can add what I know: The funder of this project is a gentleman called Rex English. He guessed that Mark might call in, and even what he might be wearing, but did not know for certain. He did not know what story might be told, but Agnes is an old and noble name, and he may have guessed she may appear as a character. I do not know if he knew your name was Agnes. I know him well but sometimes even I get left behind."

Agnes did not look reassured at all. "Well, it all still feels rather strange. But, but, I am liking the story, and Mark said yes to being with the group, and it is helpful to the children, or at least they seem to be listening, so it all seems to be coming from a good place, so maybe it is a good thing."

"One thing, though." She turned to Mark. "I don't want you to change anything in the story, especially about Agnes, just because you know I am listening. I want the story to be itself, in its own right."

"That sounds very wise to me," Emma broke in. "The best stories have their own power; we do not need to shape them too much to suit our own ends."

Agnes looked at her watch. "I must run and catch the bus." She looked at Mark. "See you next week."

Chapter 6: A Trap and the Dragon

***

"What are your names?"

"I am Agnes, and this is Edward."

"You are honoured to be named after martyrs. Have you their truth and courage?"

It was neither a question they were expecting nor wanted.

"What is *your* name?" said Agnes.

"Mine can wait."

"That's unfair," blurted out Edward.

The man came closer. And he smiled.

"You are right, that would be unfair. I will tell you. I am Lancelot, Knight of the Round Table, sworn liegeman to King Arthur."

Agnes and Edward stared.

"You look surprised," said Lancelot, conversationally.

"Why are you here?" said Edward.

"Abbess Francesca and Prior John suggested I come along. Part of the responsibility of sending someone into danger is to provide help on the way."

Agnes could not quite decide what she wanted to say next, so much was whirling round her mind. *We are not alone. Perhaps they were not wrong (or perhaps they still are). Can those Arthur stories really be true? Can this really be Lancelot?* There was a pause and she then simply said, "Is there danger?"

"There might be, and I am here to help. But I am not invincible. There may indeed be a dragon. If so, and if he sees us first, we must be careful." He paused. "Dragons kill."

"But before we go, you have not answered my question." He slowly took out his sword, rested the point on the ground with both hands gently placed on the hilt. "Have you the courage?"

There was a long pause. And then, at the same moment, Edward and Agnes replied, "I don't know."

Lancelot pulled up his sword, replaced it in the scabbard and looked at the children.

They looked at him anxiously, but secretly rather hoping that he might shake his head and send them home. Lancelot searched their eyes. He paused, as if weighing many questions, and then said: "You have answered well. We do this quest."

And as he said it Agnes and Edward felt a little stronger. It was not only the unexpected company but the fact that such a person wanted them there and felt that this might be the right quest for them.

The three walked on and the trees became closer. They had to walk in single file. Agnes first, then Edward, then Lancelot. The undergrowth got thicker, the path less easy to follow, there were glimpses of sunlight, but they became fewer as the trees became darker and closer, heavier and more entwined. They could not see very far ahead or to the sides, they moved more slowly. The minutes passed (were they becoming hours?) and the children lost track of time.

Suddenly Edward felt a sting, cried out, clasped his hand to his neck, stumbled and tripped. Agnes heard, turned her head whilst still stepping forward, and found herself falling through leaves and sticks, the ground giving way beneath her. She landed heavily; but before she had time to shout or even to think, strong hands reached for her, held her, and pulled her backwards. She could see nothing. She deliberately collapsed to the floor so her captors would be slowed down. They pulled her up, roughly, and dragged her onwards, and she realised they were in a tunnel. One of them lit a torch, but its light was faint and small and Agnes could barely see. She was still too shocked to scream. She hoped to hear running footsteps behind, of Lancelot and Edward giving chase. But she did not, and then, like a wave, fear crashed over her.

Lancelot came back from looking down the hole and crouched over Edward, examining his neck. "It was a dart, not a wasp or a bee," he said. "I wonder if they were attacking you, or wanted to distract us so that Agnes would fall into the trap. I think it was that. Hold your breath now." And before Edward had time to do anything else, Lancelot sharply pulled out the dart, which looked like a large thorn. He held it carefully, inspecting the colouring.

"Why would they want Agnes?" said Edward, and then, "It hurts, it really hurts." And there were tears in his eyes.

Lancelot continued to look carefully at the dart and then at the wound again, "I do not think it is serious; if they had wanted to kill you, they would have tipped it with a different poison. There is certainly something on the end, but it seems to be making you weak for a few minutes, rather than stopping your heart. I think they may want to capture you, as they have captured Agnes, and in that might be our opportunity. There is no sign of her in the hole."

"You could follow her."

"They would expect that and be unpleasantly ready for my arrival. Now is not the time to leave you alone. They would come for you and then would have you both. You are wounded and need to hide. Can you walk?"

Edward tried to get to his feet, but his legs gave way. Lancelot said nothing, bent down, lifted him up, put him over his shoulder and strode quickly away. He walked fast, reached slightly more open ground, and his alert hearing picked up the expected sounds behind him. He smiled grimly, reached a large oak tree, swung Edward down and put him behind it, stepped back and turned to face his pursuers.

There were two of them, short bows in their hands and long daggers in their belts. They stopped and raised their bows. "Give us the child," one called out.

"Why?" Lancelot stood, calmly, sword pointing towards the earth.

"The master wants him."

"Why?"

"Enough questions."

"Do you mean you do not know? I am surprised you take the risk of undertaking a task for someone who does not trust you with his plans."

"Enough of this, give us the child."

They moved closer, and as they did so Lancelot ran four steps to behind another tree, about six yards from where Edward was hiding. They were not quick enough to fire. And at that moment he knew he had them. They came closer, keeping both trees in their sight. "Run, Edward," he shouted, looking sideways. It was enough, his enemies, now only a few yards away, swivelled their attention to Edward's tree. Lancelot, sword in hand, rushed out and fell upon them.

The tunnel was growing brighter, the captors (Agnes guessed there were two or maybe three) pulled her into a wider space. She was flung face down on to the floor but caught a glimpse of a view of trees and grass, and even distant mountains. Perhaps the tunnel had opened to a cave? She lay flat and did not know what to do.

"What brings you to the forest?" a quiet voice asked.

"Why do you want to know?" she asked.

The slap on her face was sudden and hard. Agnes smarted.

One of the teachers at the monastery, Sister Etheldreda, had made a point of distinguishing physical from emotional reactions. "If someone hits you, then the right immediate physical reaction may be to allow the eyes to fill with tears. This does not mean you are weakened emotionally, indeed sometimes quite the opposite." And Sister Etheldreda had then made a point of saying, "Fight when you need to fight. Do not fight when you do not need to. And it is for you to decide whether you should fight emotionally or physically or both." The girls would sometimes affectionately laugh about Sister Etheldreda (even sometimes affectionally mimicking her "Indeed, sometimes quite the opposite") but at this moment, it was her voice that came back to Agnes.

She even allowed herself a slight inward smile as she remembered predictable Sister Etheldreda. *I am not alone.*

Agnes slowly got to her feet. She looked at her adversary but he was turned away.

"We are looking for the dragon," she said. And then, firmly, not pleadingly: "Don't hit me again."

Agnes could not quite work out what the person with the quiet voice looked like. He was now facing out of the cave towards the view, which Agnes could now see was broad and far. The cave entrance must be some way up the mountain; he was silhouetted. He gave a strange, deep, call. There was silence.

And then a trembling in the air.

"Little girl, you have found it," said the voice, quietly.

The sky was filled by a dark shape, growing each moment, frighteningly fast, and then the shape had great wings and it was flying straight towards the cave. It dropped and there was a loud thump as it landed heavily below. Agnes stared ahead. A noise caused her to glance behind for a moment and she saw her captors run back into the tunnel (she was right, there had been three). But the man who had been speaking stayed where he was at the entrance. And then the head of the monster appeared, filling the entrance, coming close, the cave darkening as the light was blocked. Agnes saw two cold, dark, bleak eyes looking straight in, straight at her. She stepped back.

The man stayed where he was, near the entrance, not far from the fearsome head. "You have found it, little girl. And it will attack you, not me," he said. "I am the dragon-companion."

***

Mark looked at the clock on the wall, checking he had a few more minutes. But before he could carry on, there was a question: "What is a dragon-companion?" asked Sarah. "I have not heard of one of them?"

"Dragon-companions are people who search for, and think they like, the company of dragons," said Mark. "There is something attractive in being associated with power, even when it is nasty."

"Like pretending to be a friend with the bully in the playground?"

"Yes, very much so. And sometimes the companion can be useful to the dragon, finding victims to be eaten, or to be toyed with before being burnt up, just for the pleasure of destruction. And the companion receives a measure of protection through being with the dragon, and perhaps feel good about themselves, being apparently such good friends to someone everyone else fears."

Trudy asked, "Why did you use say 'apparently'?"

"Dragons do not understand friendship as we do. Another point: sometimes a dragon-companion can end up fooling themselves that they are the dragon-keeper. But no one 'keeps' a dragon. No one controls a dragon."

"I have read stories where they are friendly," said Jason.

"And I am sure these are good stories, but they are not the same dragons as were in the old tales. The author of the stories you have read may be calling creatures dragons, but the older stories talk about different creatures, different dragons. The new approach is understandable, it can make the world seem less frightening if we think a dragon can be tamed. It helps the story feel safer. But real dragons are neither friendly nor loyal. They are driven by their greed and selfishness, by their desire to destroy. They cannot be tamed."

He looked at the three children, especially Trudy, and wondered again if he had gone too far. He smiled and said, "But they can be killed." He checked the clock again. "And now it is time to go. See you next week."

Sarah said, "I don't think I want to be a dragon-companion."

"Sometimes it takes courage to say that, to live that," said Mark. "Well done."

Miss Smith leaned forward. "Thank you so much, Mr Lind. We really should stop now."

Chapter 7: The Confrontation

***

The man stayed where he was, near the entrance, "It will attack you, not me," he said. "I am the dragon-companion. Now, answer me. Some days ago the dragon burned a knight, killed him and ate him. But, among these moments, the knight's bag slipped from his shoulder, rolled down the cliff still in flames and fell into the river. The river flows out of the forest. I am wondering if you or the little boy found the bag, or something that was in the bag, and that has brought you here." He turned towards Agnes, and she now saw the raw red and stretch of scars of many burns.

He noticed her looking. "It is not always easy being a dragon-companion; it is only for the strong and the heroic. Now, tell me, did you find the bag? Or perhaps your friend did?"

"I did not find the bag. I do not live near the river."

"So perhaps your friend." He paused. "I do not think I have further use for you. You are determined not to help me." He stepped towards her. "I decide if I am to allow the dragon his feast. Only a small feast. You are not very big or significant."

Even as the fear swept through again, Agnes wondered whether the choice no longer lay with the dragon companion (if it had ever done so). She had a feeling that the dragon made its own decisions.

She shrank back, wondering whether to try and run back to the tunnel. Were the guards still somewhere there? If she somehow got through, could she climb out of the hole the other end? It would be worth a try…

Suddenly there was a great roar. The man started, but then said: "See, he is hungry, and…" But the roar came again, and it seemed to Agnes to be a roar of challenge or anger. The man's expression changed, grew sharper; he stepped back towards her, grabbed her arm and pulled her with him towards the front of the cave. Any chance of escape was gone. The dragon's head was turned away.

And then the dragon roared a third time.

"There!" The dragon-companion shouted: "Over to the left. That is what my dragon is seeking."

And Agnes saw a figure running swiftly, not quite directly towards the cave, turning to one side or the other and whenever he disappeared from sight the dragon would roar and step forward. But the trees were close together further away from the cave and the dragon either could not, or preferred not, to leave the open ground where he had landed. He breathed bursts of fire, but still the figure was coming closer. The noise and flames were terrifying, but Agnes felt that the dragon was being cautious, as if slightly unsure.

"Why is it scared?" she asked.

The man turned and looked at her. With his left hand he was holding her arm, and he wrenched it back behind her. With his right hand he hit her across the face.

"The dragon is never scared."

Agnes, being braver than she had ever been, remembering sister Etheldreda, quietly said, "You know that is not true."

He stared at her, and there was uncertainty and fury in his eyes, and then the dragon roared again, even louder, and he turned back to look out of the cave. The figure was now at the edge of the clearing. Agnes could see more clearly; it was Lancelot.

The dragon-companion took a small step back. He loosened his grip on Agnes; she stayed where she was, watching.

The dragon, with its back to the cave, reared up, roared again, and heavily crashed forward, step by step, breathing fire. *Almost deliberately heavy, for effect,* thought Agnes. Lancelot stood. His sword in his hand but pointing to, almost resting on, the ground. His voice was clear across the clearing.

"I am not wearing armour, so you cannot bake me as if I were in an oven, and I will move too quickly to be roasted. Dragon, you must come closer to fight me or you must flee. You have been trapped, summoned wrongly here by your companion. He knew not whom he was fighting."

"You forget that I have the child," called the dragon-companion, and then, "How did you find us?"

"Your two bowmen, with a little persuasion, told me."

The dragon turned to look back at the cave, and then swiftly turned back to stare at Lancelot.

The dragon is not doubting now, he is thinking, thought Agnes, and the fear returned. *He is planning, he is weighing it all up, he is deciding how he is going to win. Real monsters are not only frightening, they are clever.*

The dragon stepped backwards. It settled again in front of the cave. The man suddenly took hold again of Agnes and swung her forward. She fell, and in an instant the claw of the dragon was pinning her to the ground.

"We want the Grail," said the dragon-companion.

"It left this land many years ago," said Lancelot. And he stepped forward, and the sword was now swinging in his hands. "If the girl is hurt, I will kill you both."

"By then it will be too late for the girl."

The dragon looked down at Agnes. All she could see in the eyes was coldness, bleak and ruthless. The claw began to press on her. She began to cry, from despair as much as from pain.

"Put down your sword," said the man in the cave.

Lancelot stopped, and looked at the dragon, then at Agnes, and then up to the mouth of the cave.

And then another voice rang out: "He cannot put down his sword." A young man, with a simple circlet around his head, walked into the glade.

"He cannot put down his sword," he repeated. "Unless I say. His sword is mine to command." He looked to the dragon-companion. "It is not yours so to do."

There was silence. The dragon was still but stayed watchful. The pressure on Agnes did not lessen but it did not increase. The man in the cave froze, and whispered: "It cannot be?"

And there was silence.

The stone missed the dragon but hit the man standing at the mouth of the cave. It was not a large stone, but it hurt enough, and he cried out.

The dragon slowly swung its great head around. And then the next stone hit it in the eye. It roared in fury and charged towards where the stone must have come from. But Edward was now behind one tree, and then to the next. The dragon paused, stretched out its neck and began to breathe deeply, and flames began to appear, longer, wider than before.

And then it stumbled. There were brief gasps of shallow fire, and then they stopped. The claw was lifted, or slid, from Agnes.

Agnes wanted to get up, to stand and run, to throw stones and fight, but the pain was too great and she could not move. Lancelot stepped forward and stood close to her, his sword again pointing to the ground, but now the blade was red. All along, it was red.

He looked up at the man in the cave.

The man hesitated. He looked at the dragon, now slumped down, blood flowing from its side. He looked further, trying to see the young man who had called out. But then he stepped to the back of the cave and ran into the tunnel. The dragon gave a painful leap, beating his wings frantically and slowly found the air. It began to fly, laboriously, noisily. *He is escaping over the trees*, thought Agnes. *He will get away.* But then there was a great, hoarse, desperate, heavy croak, and the dragon dropped. There was a great crash, and all was still.

Lancelot walked over to Agnes. "All dragons have a weak part of their armoured skin," he said. "It is not in the same place, so you have to know your dragon or guess. When the stone hit him the eye, he reared up, and so I saw a small smooth patch underneath. It seemed a likely target."

Edward came out from behind a tree. He went over to Agnes and held out his hand.

"I cannot move," said Agnes and did not try to take the hand.

Edward looked anxiously round. "Can't you help?" he said to Lancelot.

"I will do what I can, but my healing power is not that of Galahad. If he were here…"

And then they fell silent as the young man walked towards them. Lancelot dropped to one knee, motioning to Edward to do the same. Agnes tried, unsuccessfully to sit up.

The young man smiled. "Arise, noble knights. Except you, Agnes, don't move for the moment. Sometimes looking up is the same as standing."

"Will Agnes recover?" asked Edward, and he went very pale.

"It is good that you ask that question first. It is good that the sad suffering of a friend is more on your mind than the fact I named you a knight." He smiled. "We shall see what we can do to help her heal."

"Edward, you helped to kill the dragon, and you care for those in need. You are a knight." He touched his shoulder with his sword, and then reached down and prepared to do the same to Agnes, as she still lay prone on the floor.

Agnes, still gasping, said "I will try and look up."

"You, too, are a knight, you showed great courage in the cave and you remembered old truths." The young man smiled. "I, too, think Sister Etheldreda has deep wisdom."

Once again Agnes found she had too many things in her mind to know where to begin. She stayed looking up from the ground, in too much pain to sit or to stand, but her voice grew stronger. "Thank you. May I ask, who are you, and how could you do… well, what just happened? The dragon was frightened, the man was frightened. I think somehow I would have been frightened if I hadn't been hurting so much."

"I am King Arthur," the man said.

It seemed to Agnes that the silence in the glade was silent in a strange way, it was as if all nature was alive, but was quiet, in joy or anticipation, or both. And later she could not recall how long this silence lasted.

"I am glad you turned up," said Edward, at last.

"I chose to be here if help were needed. It would have been wrong of me to send Lancelot to help you if I had not ensured that Lancelot could be helped in turn. I happened to be free."

Lancelot said, "When my Lord the King Arthur says, 'I happened to be free,' some will raise a small smile. Arthur, rex quondam rexque futurus, does not 'happen to be free'. He does not simply 'turn up'. What you glimpsed there was power revealed, authority displayed, majesty shown forth, victory assured. He only does that when the need is great."

"You give the children many lessons all at once and perhaps overplay my role," said Arthur, with a smile. "Come, let us go, but before that, one thing is needed." He knelt beside Agnes, paused and put one hand lightly on the side of her shoulder. He smiled kindly and said something she did not understand. She felt a warmth and the pain left her. She scrambled to her feet and stood up.

Agnes said, "I'm ready. Thank you."

Lancelot and Arthur walked first, leading the way across the glade; Agnes and Edward walked behind. Again they joined hands, but now in fellowship and memory, not nervousness.

When they reached the edge of the trees, Edward asked, "Where are we going?"

"We are taking you home," said Arthur.

"Aren't we chasing the dragon-companion?"

"Not this time."

Lancelot said, "One adventure at a time is enough."

And Agnes was asking herself: *How did he know about Sister Etheldreda?*

***

"Will they go back for the dragon-companion?" asked Sarah.

"Perhaps," said Mark. "We do not see every chapter of the story all at once."

"At least they got rid of the dragon," said Trudy.

"They did indeed," said Mark. He paused and then asked: "Who, for you, is the main character in the story?"

The three children looked at each other, unsure about committing, and adjusting to being involved in a different way. No one said anything, and then Mr Cook, sitting behind, said, "May I go first? Mine would be Brother James. He is the one teaching and guiding Edward."

"It is really difficult," said Sarah. "I think it would be Agnes. She is very brave."

"Edward for me," said Trudy. "He threw the stones."

"Well, Lancelot was there for them, and killed the dragon, so I will go for him," said Jason.

There was a brief silence.

"Well," said Miss Smith. "I guess it is my turn. I am torn between Edward's mother and Sir Lancelot, the dragon-companion (would it not be interesting to know why he had ended up where he was?) and Abbess Francesca."

"That's cheating," said Jason, gleefully and affectionately. "You can't have four!"

"Perhaps," said Mark gently and clearly, bringing the attention back to his voice, "perhaps we would choose different characters at different times, depending on how we are feeling.

"Isn't it interesting that as soon as someone is named, we can see their role in the story in a new way? Is there a significance there that we had not spotted before?"

"May I say, Mr Lind," said Mr Cook. "What this reminds us, is that each person in the story has an important role to play. No one is unimportant."

"Thank you, Mr Cook, that is very helpful. I think that is a good place to finish." He checked the clock. "We should stop now. See you next week."

The children and teachers left, and Agnes came over from the reception desk. "We can close up now and see if anyone is in the park?"

Chapter 8: Agnes Tells Her Story

The folly seemed rather full. Jenny Loss, Mr English, Emma and Jane were already there. And someone whom Agnes did not know.

He stood. "Agnes, it is an honour to see you, my name is Gary Ladd. Mark, it is good to see you again."

Agnes was rather tongue-tied. She sensed a deep power and peace in this new person. She later described it to a friend as "You know, being with someone who has found what they are looking for and are content." 'Like being in a nice house?' the friend had ventured. Agnes then said, "Sort of but no, much bigger than that. In a different league."

Mark said, "Gary, I hoped we would meet again. I felt it likely we would." And the two old friends smiled and clasped hands.

Mr English looked around the semi-circle. He sat in the middle, facing the entrance, looking out into the park. "It is a long time since some of us sat together. It is good to welcome Agnes this afternoon."

Agnes shifted nervously. "This is all rather more than I expected."

Jenny said kindly, "Agnes, is there something on your mind? You look as if you want to ask something."

"Oh dear, I have such an expressive face, people have always said. Yes please. Mark asked which character was the most important in the story, and he was nice about what they all said, although Miss Smith did not really give an answer at all, but no one said the figure who appeared at the end, the one who the dragon-companion called Arthur."

Mr English smiled. "He quite often gets left out. He does not mind."

"I think it was a shame, anyway," said Agnes, "and then, like the children, I wanted to know what would happen to the dragon-companion."

Mark said, "I wanted to wrap up the story for the day. Edward and Agnes had to be got home. And perhaps sometimes simply, as Lancelot said, one quest at a time is enough."

Agnes said: "I have another question, too. In the story, Arthur appears to have such power that, when he chooses, he can do anything if the need is great enough. But is that really true?"

"No, it is not true," said Mr English. "He is not all-powerful. He can be defeated."

"Then why put it in the story?" Agnes asked, feeling bolder now.

"Because," said Mark, "sometimes we need to know that the dragons will be defeated. There was also another reason to include him; I wanted to make the point that we all need help. Edward and Agnes need Lancelot and Lancelot (even Lancelot!) needs help. We are never asked to do something for which the help is not provided."

Emma said: "At the end of time, some of us believe that all dragons will be defeated, but we need to avoid giving false hope now. It is a difficult balance." She went on, more quietly: "I know the pain of feeling that the dragons are winning; but I think children know that a story is different, and it may give them an encouraging glimpse of things being put right. I am not sure I would call it false hope. Sometimes they just need the glimpse. Would we want stories where the dragons always win?"

Jenny brought things back. "Agnes, it is very good to have you with us, tell us what part of the story unsettled you. I think that now is the time."

Agnes looked around at the faces, decided she would be honest, and said: "The part when the dragon claw was pressing down."

"Tell us what is on your mind," said Jenny, and sat back, as if trying to make herself comfortable (not easy in a stone folly), as if saying, take as much time as you want. Agnes breathed deeply, and then began:

"I have not told anyone this. It happened when I was in school. I was fourteen, so about ten years ago. My school was St George's, not far from here. I will try and tell the story. I have never told it before but have practised it many times in my head and have found it easier to tell it as if I am a character in it, not the narrator, so I will tell it in the third person, so I can be more detached. I want to try and remember it clearly."

Jane gave a big encouraging smile.

Gary said, "We thank you for your trust. Tell the story as you wish."

***

"I left my watch in the changing room, won't be a minute," said Agnes.

She rushed away back across the playground, went into the changing room, searched around in the corner where she had earlier changed for her games lesson, found the watch, and then noticed Freda's hockey stick lying under a bench. She wondered if she took it now whether she would catch up with her before she left school and decided it was worth a try. She picked it up, ran out and looked around the playground. There was no sign of Freda, she must have gone. Agnes was not sure what to do, she was in a hurry herself, her bus would be going soon.

She ran to her classroom, opened her own locker, put the hockey stick in, and rushed for the bus.

The next morning her form-teacher said she was not to go to assembly with the others but needed to see the Headmaster, Mr Edge. She wondered what this might be – some praise for a recent piece of work? An invitation to be a prefect?

"Sit down, Agnes," Mr Edge said. "Let me be absolutely clear, we know what you have done. It will not help you to deny it. Several people saw you."

Agnes wondered what was wrong. She had never been in trouble at school before. She felt as if she was suddenly part of a different world, as if now the sun was shadowed. This was a side of school-life she had never known.

She did not know where to begin. "I do not understand. What did someone see me do?" she asked cautiously.

"You are sounding over-careful and defensive," said Mr Edge, sharply. "That is revealing and interesting. Don't try and hide the truth from me. No, of course they did not see you actually take it, but they saw you run with it, and then you must have hidden it."

Agnes' mind was slowly catching up. "Was this the hockey stick? I was trying to return it to Freda."

"It was Freda that reported it missing, after she went to look this morning. She made no mention of asking you to return it, or of you having it at all."

Agnes looked up and saw the eyes were cold.

"But she wouldn't have known. I was going to tell her this morning. Why don't you believe me?" she blurted out.

"Don't be impertinent. We have to be very careful about theft, very rigorous. You need to learn a lesson, and an example made for the good of the school. I have my policies to follow, our reputation to protect." And he tapped a piece of paper on his desk.

"I put it in my locker in the classroom. It'll still be there."

"So, deliberately hiding it in your locker? But it does not matter if it is there or not, you took something without the owner's permission. And it hardly clears you of your guilt that it may be in your locker." Mr Edge sighed. "Not a very clever place to hide it, if I may say."

"I was trying to be helpful," said Agnes, desperately.

The eyes stayed cold. "Of course you would say that now."

Agnes crumpled. And she realised she could not speak. Everything was changing. Yesterday she had been at the heart of things, doing her best as well as she could, part of school-life, smiled at by teachers in the corridor. She was now in a space she had only heard about, one that badly-behaved pupils knew well. And now she was one of those. It was as if she had suddenly become the enemy.

***

Agnes stopped speaking. It was one of those large silences when everyone knew that the first words spoken would be important, and it would be important who said them.

"Sweetheart, you are not the enemy," Mr English said.

"What happened next?" asked Mark.

"They suspended me from school for a week. And told me everything would be back to normal when I returned. But of course it wasn't. I had been labelled a thief. It was a horrible rest of term, and I decided I had to leave. But then the school said they would have to tell my next school what I had done, and I realised I could only go somewhere that was desperate for numbers. If you could pick and choose, why would you accept a thief? So I had to stay."

"But you hadn't done anything wrong," said Jane.

"I should have called Freda that first night to tell her I had her hockey stick. But I was out that evening, and then wanted to surprise her happily in the morning. I got everything wrong."

"You have gone from 'She' to 'I'," said Rex English. "That may sometimes be a good thing. But we need be as truthful as we can, not to deepen the wound with unjustified pain: Agnes, you did not get everything wrong. In truth, you got very little wrong. You were unjustly punished."

"And it felt like being crushed by a dragon's claw?" said Jane. "And there was no Edward or Lancelot or Arthur to remove the pressure, to put right the injustice?"

Agnes sat still and then put her head in her hands. When she looked up, the tears were there, but she said: "There were some Edwards, trying to help, to make the point, to distract the dragon, or even to make him change his mind. Freda was one of them, she tried to say something to Mr Edge, saying she had only reported a lost hockey stick, that she had never meant me to get into trouble."

"The pressure of the dragon's claw has stayed with you dear Agnes," said Mr English. "The time for relief is now." Mr English got up and stood before Agnes, paused, and put one hand lightly on the side of her shoulder. "It is a great wrong to be unfairly treated, you have been bruised by injustice, but you have not been broken. Begin your new chapter, step free from Mr Edge. His power is less than you think."

There was quiet for a moment. Agnes realised that the new person, Gary, had not said anything. For some reason she looked across at him.

He bowed his head briefly, and then smiled at her. "Agnes, I honour you. When you picked up the hockey-stick to try and help Freda, you were acting out of kindness. And of sacrifice – you may have missed your bus. Therefore it was a good and noble act. It has been, is, and will be, honoured in the deeper places, whatever the results and pain in this misunderstanding and careless world turned out to be."

Agnes realised her mouth was open. She closed it quickly, shook herself slightly and said, "Well, that was a bit more than I bargained for!"

Agnes had left the folly.

"Did Mr Edge take over from Mr Moore?" asked Mark. "Why did he want to punish Agnes so much?"

"Yes he did," said Jenny. "He was the next Headmaster. I had stopped working at St George's by then but kept in touch with old colleagues. He was not as clearly linked to the Le Fays as Ed Moore had been, but somehow their influence was felt in different ways. There was a ruthless insistence on procedures (always apparently with the best of intentions). Whatever the right or wrong, whatever the human need at the heart of the event, if the right procedure or policy was not followed or, even more importantly in the eyes of Mr Edge, not *seen* to be followed, then someone would suffer. My guess is that he did not want to punish Agnes particularly, he was simply over-cautious about his reputation as a 'firm' leader. Strange to say, if he had been a stronger leader, he might not have needed to be so firm."

"He might not have realised Agnes was being crushed," said Emma.

"I think he would never have thought to ask himself that question. And if he had known he would have seen it as an acceptable cost." Jenny's voice became slightly harder. "He did a great evil. She is still suffering all these years later. This is what injustice and unkindness can do."

"Ultimately he will have damaged himself more than Agnes," said Gary. "She is on the side of the light."

"Would it be too contrived to say that he was the claw, but someone else was the dragon?" said Mark.

"Much too contrived," said Jane, "but quite fun!"

Chapter 9: An Unexpected Task

Next Monday Mark was back in the library. He paused at the desk on his way in. Before he spoke, Agnes said quietly. "Thank you, I am okay." He moved over to the story-telling area and sat down. Trudy, Jason and Sarah were there on the cushions, Mr Cook and Miss Smith were sitting behind.

***

Edward and Agnes sat next to each other and looked out into the cloister garden. It was a cloudy day and the stone was light brown more than golden, but the sense of peace was the same as ever. Brother James had asked if Agnes could join them that afternoon, there was a task for them to do.

"Do you think we will be sent into the forest again, perhaps to see if we can capture the dragon-companion?" Edward wondered.

"I hope not," said Agnes. "But if we are, we are."

Prior John came through a door at the end of the cloister and walked towards them. He paused in front of them and smiled in welcome. "I feel it would be good if you helped our local hermit. There is bread and cheese in this bag, I would like you to take it to him in the east of the forest."

"Why?" asked Edward. Inwardly he was relieved that they were not chasing dragons again, but it seemed rather a tame task.

"We would not want him to go hungry."

"No, I didn't mean that, I meant: why us? I thought we were…"

He paused, realising what the end of the sentence might sound like if it came out.

Prior John did not quite frown, but his smile grew slightly less.

"It is a noble task to take food to anyone, even for a knight – especially for a knight. And the hermit's company is always a blessing. Taking food to a hermit is sometimes as important as fighting a dragon."

Edward nodded, feeling rather ashamed of himself.

Prior John continued, and his voice was now gentler: "It is a narrow path and his cave is not easy to find, Brother James will go with you. He is waiting outside the gate." And then: "This is why you are good knights: you are willing to learn."

"Do you often see the hermit?" Agnes asked Brother James, when they were on their way.

"Not often. But sometimes I come across him. If I realise I have not seen him for some time, I go and find him."

"Why?"

"I like talking with him, he always makes me think. I happen to know that he also makes many other people think as well, and it seems good, is part of our duty as a monastery, to ensure he is looked after."

"I thought hermits stay in the same place," said Edward.

"Some do, others stay on the move. Being a hermit is not about *where* you are, it is about *who* you are. It is about knowing what it is to withdraw from some of the pressures of the world; it is not possible to withdraw from all of them, nor would we wish to do so."

Agnes noticed the "we". Brother James noticed the noticing and smiled. He said simply: "Yes, in a different way. I, too, am one."

Edward said, "Brother James. I used to come into the forest for fun. I used to climb and swim, watch out for the rabbits and the badgers, imagine adventures. It feels no longer somewhere to play, but a place where I have to *do* things, where there is danger or duty."

"Dear Edward, perhaps it is both places. And perhaps you always knew that part of the fun of the playing was that the forest is larger and deeper. In the same way as playing in the sand on a beach with the waves of the vast and mysterious sea nearby, is different from playing in a patch of sand at the side of a stream. And in your stories and explorations, were you not giving yourself tasks? Did you not sometimes imagine danger? But you are right, time has passed. Responsibilities are come upon you. But keep hold of the desire to play. To hold the play and the tasks, the joy and the duty, together, well-balanced and well-matched, is a fine calling."

Agnes asked: "May we go to the beach sometime? I have never been to the sea."

"Nor have I," said Edward.

Brother James smiled. "Perhaps one day."

The path was one that Edward had not known before, Brother James led the way. The children increasingly glanced from side to side, and Agnes realised she was becoming nervous. The path was wide enough for the children to walk together and Edward could sense her feelings.

"Brother James," he said. "May we stop for a moment?"

"Of course. There is room for us to sit in that patch of grass over there."

"No, I would like to stay on the path," said Agnes, quickly. "Brother James, how much do you know of our last journey in the forest?"

"Agnes, do not worry, the dragon-companion is not here. You are right to check, this is the same forest, and the memories are painful, but you can travel this path in peace. One of the reasons why a visit to the hermit was felt to be good, was to reassure you that much of the forest is safe. This journey need not remind you of evil hours. Perhaps, even more, it can remind you that the dragon is dead, and that both of you were part of that victory. When holding memories, recall the good as well as the bad. Prior John would not want you to avoid the forest for the rest of your life."

"So it is no longer dangerous?" asked Edward, as Agnes continued to look downwards, gazing uncertainly at the ground.

"Nowhere is completely safe, and the forest is certainly not, there are other dangers than dragons here. But we weigh up the risks of danger, we note what protection is offered, we stay as far as we can to the safe paths, we decide on the trustworthiness of the one who asked us to make the journey."

He smiled and lightened his tone. "And the hermit needs his bread and cheese."

Agnes said, "When Lancelot first met us, he asked if we had courage. I thought that was a frightening question, I now see it was a wise one, I am ready to carry on."

"It is a very wise question, and it is wise to ask it more than once."

He smiled, and the three companions continued along the path.

***

"That was short," said Jason, looking at the clock. "And not very much happened. Can we have something more? We have time?"

"We could discuss…" Mark began.

"I don't want to discuss again, we do that all the time at school. This library-time is meant to be different," said Sarah.

Mark smiled. "I should have asked you this in the first week, but perhaps we know each other better, trust each other more, and so now is a good time to ask: What is this library-time for?"

He noted some nervousness and hurried on: "I don't mean, why were you asked to be here. I mean what the time needs to be, for you."

There was a slightly embarrassed silence, and then Mr Cook said, "It is the one time of the week when nothing is demanded of us. When we simply receive. Mr Lind, one or two of the pupils have, I think, been telling their friends they come here. And their friends now want to come along. We could fill the whole library with those who have stopped me in the corridor and asked if, for half-an-hour each week, they can sit on cushions and hear stories told. Nothing more."

There was quiet for several moments.

"Thank you Mr Cook, and thank you Sarah, that was very helpful. No discussion then today, but perhaps just a few moments when we silently ask ourselves whether anything did happen in today's chapter."

And so they did. And Mark sensed that the mood had relaxed and now felt safe, and wondered if Mr Cook's choice of pronoun was one of the things that had happened that afternoon.

Chapter 10: The Wisdom of the Hermit

***

They continued along the path.

The hermit was standing in the entrance of a cave. He was short, and round, and his eyes were sparkling. The children immediately felt he was friendly, and relaxed.

"Welcome fair and noble friend, Brother James, and welcome to your two companions."

"They are Agnes and Edward. And they have brought food."

"That is kind of them, what use is a hungry hermit?" And he smiled broadly. "Especially as they may have been hoping for a more exciting adventure than bringing lunch to a hermit in a cave? Accept my gratitude. It is perhaps not the same as hearing songs of triumph after a great quest, but it is offered whole-heartedly, nonetheless."

Agnes stepped forward, gave a little bow, and handed over the little bag of bread and cheese. "Perhaps there is a song of triumph for every good deed."

The hermit threw his head back and laughed and then looked carefully at her. "You have wisdom in your eyes," he said, "My name is Cuthbert."

"I am Agnes, and this is Edward."

"I know, I know, even an old hermit" (*he is not old at all*, thought the children) "can remember the words of Brother

James. Whose every word we should hear like the hawk – James, do hawks hear as well as they can see? I can never remember – Edward, is he trying to teach you Latin?

"Sir, he is. And he describes the great cities to me: Athens, Rome, Jerusalem."

"Learn well, learn well, dive deep into the riches. But remember that a city's true greatness is the quality of those who live there. And remember that greatness needs to be renewed each day, lest it become stale and tired. Now, Agnes, what do you learn?"

"I live in a monastery, and I, too, am learning my words. I like to learn songs, as well of course as my psalms and prayers."

"To know that the world is a song or a poem, to know life needs rhythm and rhyme (however hidden), that is a great gift, my lady."

Agnes blushed a little.

Cuthbert smiled. "My words need not be felt as over-solemn, sit lightly my friends, but know that they are all deeply felt. I must show you around, do come in."

The cave widened once they were through the entrance. They found themselves in an area the size of a large room. And around this space were seven more entrances carved into the rock. "I shall show you round," said Cuthbert. "Or would you like to share food first? You have journeyed long. It is a noble thing to eat together, a truth I hold close to my heart, as you can see." And he laughed again.

Brother James said, "We should not stay too long. Show us your home first, and then we shall eat."

Cuthbert nodded. "First I should explain this hall. This is where I eat (when I am allowed to, Brother James!) And I eat here, in sight of the entrance, in case a passing friend wants to join me."

"Do many friends come here?" asked Agnes.

"They do," answered Cuthbert. "Sometimes I have met them before, sometimes I have not. To eat, and sometimes to eat with others, is always a precious and honourable action." He looked quite serious at this point.

"Why so special?" asked Agnes.

"Eating is an act of humility and thanksgiving; it reminds us that we need help and strength to keep going. Eating with another is an act of friendship and trust. We are vulnerable when we are eating. A hand holding bread cannot be holding a knife."

"But the other hand might be, there have been many murders across the meal table," said Brother James.

"You are right. The vulnerability can be a disguise. The sacredness of the shared eating can be violated. Likewise, gratitude for food can be turned to greed." His expression saddened for a moment. "Do I dare have two crusts on my table when you have none on yours?"

He paused. "Come, let me show you further in."

"Each of these entrances lead to a different room, and I visit them every day. They are all rather small so it would be rather a squash if we went in together. They are smaller spaces leading from, and giving strength to, the larger, welcoming, first space.

"This is one of my favourites. It is where I rest, and it is where I sleep." The children looked in and saw a plain and simple bed. "Resting and sleeping are not always the same thing," Cuthbert said. "But I use this room for both activities."

He pointed to the next one. "Here we have my learning room." The children, peering in, could see a small book lying on the floor beside a chair. "The book changes from time to time," he murmured. "Friends kindly bring me new ones." At this point he looked rather pointedly back at Brother James, who smiled. "Next time, dear Cuthbert, next time."

"Then this is my room to create." Propped up in one corner was a musical instrument, some sort of lyre, Agnes thought. On a table was a clay pot, with decorations running round the outside.

They looked into the fourth room. There were tiny faces drawn around the walls, with space for more. The children looked at the hermit enquiringly. "This is my room where I go to remember people in need. I draw a face each time someone comes to mind."

"Is that why some look like old drawings and some are fresh?" asked Edward.

The hermit nodded. "That one down there, I drew her yesterday."

"Why faces, and not names?" asked Agnes.

"I sometimes have visitors, it is right to keep my prayerful intentions private. I draw so badly that no one is recognisable." He then brightened. "Make the most of weaknesses. They are a gift and have their uses! Needless to say, one of the faces is mine. I am often in need, as much as anyone else. Some of the faces are made up; I hear about a tragedy in another land, I imagine what the suffering person may look like, and I draw a face."

"Why are they so small?" asked Agnes.

"I do not know how many people I will meet, and the wall may fill up too soon. There may be several years left in me, I need to leave space."

There was a pause; it seemed to the children rather a solemn thing to say.

"Will you draw us?" asked Edward.

"Would you like me to?"

"Yes," both children said at once.

"It would be an honour to do so." And Cuthbert looked steadily at their faces, as if holding them in his mind. "I will draw them this afternoon."

"And the fifth room?" asked Agnes.

"It is for the glory of everyday tasks. There you might find a shirt to be mended, an axe to be sharpened, or a pot waiting to be taken to the stream to be washed."

He moved to the next room. "And this is my room of thanksgiving." The children peered in and again there were faces on the wall, but also landscapes and buildings, animals and flowers. "I come in here and I am thankful."

"And you draw the person or place or the moment?" asked Agnes.

Cuthbert nodded. "I try to. And it is good to look back at older drawings, and to be thankful for them, again. And often the same faces will be in this room as in the fourth room."

"Last one," he said. And looking in they saw three marks, going across the wall, about a yard between each one. "Do you want to guess?" Cuthbert asked.

Edward and Agnes shook their heads. "I do not know," said Edward.

"This is my bringing-together room. I think about the past, the present and the future. Those are the three marks. I try and hold what has happened, and how it has affected me. I try and consider what is happening now, and what my role in it is to be. I try and decide what plans may need to be made for the future, whilst knowing that the future will be full of surprises. It becomes the room where I see things more broadly, and that can help relieve the pressure."

Agnes looked up. "How?"

"Because it reminds me that whenever I feel, or have felt, oppressed or joyful, that this is a moment in a much longer story. The journey is bigger than one pausing-place, there are many views along the way."

Brother James had stayed in the welcome space while they had been looking into the rooms. When he saw they had finished he said, "I have successfully guarded the food! Now, master hermit, may we be part of your hospitality?"

"You are welcome, and, how can I say no to a hungry monk?" said Cuthbert.

The four sat round the table and opened the bag. There was more than enough bread and cheese. Edward was handed a bucket made of leather and was asked to go to the stream and he brought back water. Cuthbert dipped a jug into the bucket and they all had water from small cups. "Made by me," said Cuthbert.

"In the third room or the fifth room?" said Agnes.

There was a pause, and the hermit said, thoughtfully, "In both, two from one, two from the other. It was not planned, it happened that way." He looked at her keenly.

"I can't tell the difference, about the cups, I mean," said Edward.

"Nor can I, now," said Cuthbert.

"Seven rooms," said Edward. "One for each day of the week."

"Very true, very true," said Cuthbert. "But I visit each room once a day, and so I have a rhythm of the day as well a rhythm of a week."

"And we do not forget this welcome hall," said Brother James. "Right at the centre."

There was another pause, and suddenly Cuthbert slapped his hand on the table. "Ah, we are all looking much too solemn and serious. A feast is a place for laughter as well as learned ponderings, of guffaws as well as grave thoughts. We need a tale – let me sing the great and tragic song of The Weasels and The Food. Agnes, run and fetch the lyre."

The lyre was fetched. Cuthbert pushed his stool back, took the lyre, winced as he heard the tuning, fiddled with the pegs, and then began.

The Weasels were a-slithering and plotting evil deeds
Deep among the rotten roots of old decaying trees.
They schemed and smirked and planned, with greed in thieving hearts
"We know a store of food, kept by a hermit in these parts."

"We do not wish to work, and do not wish to pay.
We want to steal and grab, we want the lazy way.
Let's find that hermit's cave, and sneak behind his back
And empty all his cupboards, his boxes and his sacks."

But when those wily weasels, reached at last the hermit's cave
He was standing in the entrance, much to their dismay.
"Let's rush him all at once, he'll run away for sure.
And if not that, then gladly, we'll knock him to the floor."

But what those rascals had forgot was the fine and rounded shape
Of the tummy of the hermit who stood across the gap
They charged and leapt and shouted, but bounced back to the ground
It's tough to pass a hermit when he is quite so round

Deep among the rotten roots of old decaying trees
The Weasels were a-grumbling and whining through their teeth
They snarled and cursed each other, and none would take the blame
And in his cave the hermit smiled, and helped himself to cake.

After they had eaten it was time to go. Brother James needed to be back at the monastery to fulfil his duties.

***

"Thank you all very much," said Mark, "We should leave it there for today."

"That seemed a sudden ending. I liked the hermit's poem. And then it all just stopped. Did you run out of time?" Said Sarah.

Jason put up his hand. "Mr Lind, you never told us what happened to the Grailstand. Can you put that into the story?"

Mark smiled. "I will see what I can do next week."

Sarah said, "I would have liked to have heard how the hermit said goodbye. He seemed fun."

Mark said: "So would I. But when I was thinking about this chapter, the hermit suddenly became significant to the children, and I was not quite sure why or how, and then I could not find the right words for the ending. Perhaps if I told it again, I would be clearer in my mind what to do with him."

Chapter 11: The Grailstand is Sought

It was next Monday.

***

When Edward arrived home after he and Agnes had met the hermit, he found his mother sitting quietly outside their little house. She heard his footsteps and looked up. And he knew something was wrong.

"I do not know what has happened," she said. "Before I left to collect the water from the well I thought I had tidied everything, but when I came back, it was a mess. Either I am becoming forgetful, or I had not tidied properly, or someone has been here, looking for something."

Edward sat next to her for a while on the bench. And then, slowly, went inside. They had very few possessions, but each one mattered and had a story to tell, and it seemed strange not to see them in their places, discomforting to see them scattered on the earth floor. He thought for a moment, went back outside and then round the back. There, a few moments of digging answered his unspoken question, the Grailstand was still there, hidden where he had buried it. He picked it up and returned to his mother. "I wonder if someone was looking for this."

She thought for a while, and then said, "I think it should go to the monastery."

"Yes," said Edward. "I suppose you are right. But I quite like having it here. And it might be valuable, perhaps we could become rich."

"I do not think it was made to make people rich with money," she replied. "And if it did, it would be a twisting of its purpose, and it would not make us happy."

"Let's clear up the house, and tomorrow I will take it to Brother James." But there was a slight reluctance in his voice.

However, the next morning Edward knew he must fulfil his promise and he set off to the monastery, with the Grailstand in a little bag. He decided to walk along the river, as he had done so in the opposite direction when he had first seen it glinting in the sunlight. He paused at the same spot, standing at the riverside for some minutes. Finally he turned to continue down the path but there was someone barring his way.

He must have been watching from behind the trees, and moved quickly while I was looking at the river. Why did I stop? Why did I take the long way? Edward recognised the person. He had last seen him standing in mouth of the cave, it was the dragon-companion.

"Give me the bag," the man said.

"No," said Edward. And began to move, hoping to get clear. But the dragon-companion hit him, very hard. And Edward fell heavily to the ground.

When Edward opened his eyes he groaned, and then slowly, very slowly, got up. The bag was gone, and so was the man. His face hurt, and he wondered if his nose was broken. He decided he should go on to the monastery; he was too miserable to go straight home, and he knew the monks were good with the injured as well as the sick.

He walked slowly on, and it was a relief when he was sitting in the cloisters. The gatekeeper had alerted Brother James, who came hurrying to meet him.

"Before anything else, let us take you to the infirmary. Brother Luke will have a good look and clean you up."

Edward did not move. Brother James gently took him by the hand and led him away. Brother Luke washed his face with warm and soothing water – "A herb or two in that, I expect," said Brother James – and announced that he did not think the nose was broken, but there would come considerable bruising around his eye. Edward realised that *so much* had been hurting that he had not been able to tell *what* had been hurting.

They returned to the Cloister, and Prior John was waiting. Agnes was there, too.

"I asked Abbess Francesca if Agnes could join us, because there are times when we need to be with friends," said Prior John.

Edward had mixed feelings, he liked Agnes, but felt his morning had been a story of failure and he guessed he looked as rough as he felt. He stayed where he was, head bowed.

"The dragon-companion has got the Grailstand. It is my fault. I did not come straight here. Deep down, I wanted to keep it, and now I have lost it for all of us, and to our enemy. There, I have been completely honest. And I am so sorry, and I feel very bad."

"It may not be as bad as you think," said Prior John.

"But he has got the Grailstand," said Edward, bleakly.

"It has no power; it will not do him any good. He may even have done us a favour. Such things can acquire an importance, a sacredness that was not originally there. What would have happened if we had found the table on which the Grailstand sat, or the straw under the table, or the mouse that ran across the straw, or the cat that chased the mouse? Does everything then have to be kept and stored and preserved? If you had brought it here, we would have honoured and treasured it, and in this generation we would have held our reverence in balance. But future generations may have then over-endowed it with unnecessary significance. It would have been pleasing and interesting to have it here, but we cannot hold on to everything.

"The dragon-companion will be disappointed. It will bring him nothing except the reminder that he is far from the Grail, and in stealing this, and in hurting you, he has moved further away. There is sadness there, too.

"And, dear Edward, remember the hold it was beginning to have, even on you. Perhaps it was better for all of us that it was lost."

"I don't feel very proud of myself."

"That is always a good sign," said Abbess Francesca with a smile. "It would be much more worrying if you did. But you must be fair to give credit where it is due. You did agree, despite your desire, despite your decision to take a strange route, to bring the Grailstand back. That is good news. You are a noble knight."

***

Jason said, "I would have liked it if he had fought back, and won, and kept the Grailstand safe. I don't like it when the wrong people win."

"It is how it happens sometimes," said Mark. "Edward made mistakes, but in his heart he knew what was right. The important thing is for the loss or shame not to crush us too much, nor to make us feel less worthy than we should." He paused and said slowly: "Prior John was not worried."

"Why was he *sad* about the dragon-companion?" asked Sarah.

"Perhaps we shall learn next week," said Mark. "And now it really is time to go."

Chapter 12: Restoration

"I have been thinking, Mr Lind," said Sarah. "Perhaps Prior John was sad because he cares for the dragon-companion; perhaps he knew him before he went bad. Perhaps – this would make a good story – perhaps they are distant relations!"

"Or," said Trudy, "he was scared that the disappointment would make him, the dragon-companion I mean, even more cross and dangerous."

Miss Smith leaned forward. "Which, Mr Lind, will it be?"

Mark smiled, "Let's see what happens."

***

On their way home, Agnes and Edward had been having the same discussion. They realised that one reason why they did not know the reason for the sadness was that Prior John's face gave little away when he was speaking. "He just, somehow, always sounds *thoughtful*," said Edward.

"Hard to tell if worried or sad, or quietly pleased," agreed Agnes.

"That's sometimes *really* annoying!" said Edward, and they laughed.

What they did not know was that later the same day, in Agnes' monastery, a discussion was happening about the Grailstand between Abbess Francesca and Prior John.

"The Grailstand, if it is that, does not matter in itself. It is people's reactions that are the issue, that can be dangerous," said John.

"Then to be safe we should retrieve the Grailstand," said Francesca. "And we should be reluctant to send the children. That would not be safe. There is one who is not tainted by ambition or greed, who has proved his worth. The Grail is on his heart, and I think he will respond. We shall need to ask Arthur to ask him."

John nodded. "These are wise words, I agree. I will send a message."

***

"Who do they want to send?" asked Trudy. "Why do they not just say? Or is it you, Mr Lind, trying to keep us guessing, whilst we all know it is Lancelot."

"Lancelot would have been a good choice," said Mark, "but there was another knight they had in mind. I am going to keep you guessing just a little longer, and tell the story as it unfolded, or, rather, as Edward and Agnes heard it."

***

A few days later Agnes and Edward were sitting in the cloister and Brother James was telling them the story of the geese that saved Rome. They had heard it before, but enjoyed it once more, resting in the late afternoon sun. Brother James looked up. "Someone is joining us. Ah, I think we should stand."

A figure came through the archway at the end of the cloister and walked towards them. He was of average height, simply dressed, and wearing a cloak. He looked rather ordinary. He stopped and bowed towards them.

"Brother James, I honour you as a faithful teacher. Edward and Agnes, I honour you for your courage." He smiled and shrugged. "I was told to say that by my companion Lancelot." There was another pause, and he then said: "I have brought back the Grailstand. And it is indeed the holder of the Grail, it is now safe with Prior John."

The children looked at him and were not sure what to say. Edward was thinking that he would quite like to see the Grailstand again and was wondering how he could ask. But their attention was caught by the two figures who now followed into the cloister. One was Prior John, the other had his face covered by a scarf.

The person spoke again. "My name is Galahad, I am a knight. I am a guardian of the Grail."

"The Grailstand I have brought back, but here is someone who is a much richer treasure." And he turned to the veiled man, who reached up and unwrapped the scarf from his face.

It was the dragon-companion.

Agnes did not feel as scared as she might have imagined she would have been if she had known she would be faced with him again. And she felt (and it brought an inner smile) a quick memory of Sister Etheldreda: "*Indeed, sometimes quite the opposite.*"

Edward was unsure, slightly angry and very confused; he had noted Galahad's words about treasure, and he did not understand.

"Your scars are fading, I can hardly see them," said Agnes, slowly.

"I have been told that is part of what happens. Things can be reversed," replied the dragon-companion. "I have even remembered my name, which for many years was lost."

"What is your name?" asked Edward.

"Felix."

"That means 'happy', I think," said Edward.

The man smiled. "And so once I was, and now might be again."

"How did all this happen?" asked Agnes.

"Let us sit," said Prior John, "and hear the story. Who shall do the telling?"

"I think it is mine to tell," said Felix, and Prior John smiled and nodded.

"Many years ago I was enticed into tying my life and fortune to that of the dragon (it does not now matter how, but there is a story to tell there, too). This gave me power. But behind the dragon I sensed something bigger, a larger struggle going on, and it was not long before I was told that I must look out for anything connected to the Grail. Once I had taken the Grailstand – Edward, I am sorry for what I did – I felt I was beginning to get close. But it sat on my shelf (I live in another cave, not the one you were in, Agnes, and I am sorry for that, too.) and I realised it was doing nothing for me. I was looking for a new dragon, but there are very few left and the killing of the old one had made me realise that they were not as all-powerful as I had once thought."

"When Galahad appeared in the entrance to my cave, he looked so ordinary that I felt he was no threat. I was surprised he had found me but felt in no danger. My knife was close at hand. I told him he was lost and should make his way home. He said that this was sound counsel, and that more should hear it, and he stayed standing at the entrance. I reached for my knife and stood."

"*I have come for the Grailstand, he said. "It is not yours to keep. And I have come for you. Felix, it is time to come home."*

"I do not know if it was the words he said (it was the first time I had heard my name for many, many, years), or the way he said them, but I felt strength leave me and I collapsed."

"We talked long into the night, we talked about many things, and now here I am."

***

"So he simply appears? Welcomed to the monastery? No punishment?" said Trudy.

"We do not know what Galahad said to him," said Mark.

"That seems so unfair."

"Galahad and the Grail are mixed up in mercy. Galahad can exercise the power of mercy more effectively than most."

Trudy went very quiet and tense, and there was a slightly awkward silence.

Sarah broke in, kindly: "May I say something that is different, but has been on my mind for weeks? In the story, Edward and Agnes had never been to the sea. I have only been to the sea once, when I was young, and I paddled in the waves. It all seemed so large and clean and, and, mysterious, but I remember most the feel of the water over my toes, and the little rock pools. Can you do something about the sea?"

"Well, I had not been thinking about that. You listened well to have spotted that."

"But you mentioned it, so it must have mattered. I think you are a careful storyteller," said Sarah.

Mark looked at her thoughtfully. "Sometimes I say things that just seem to fit, even if I think there is little significance beneath it. But you have made me think. Perhaps my choice of filler-phrases, if I may call them that, have more meaning than I realise. Let's see what we can do next week."

"I still think something should have happened to the dragon-companion," said Trudy, and there was real anger in her voice.

"So do I," said Miss Smith, "because I think we should remember the dragons who may have needed him. We only have the Prior's word for it that all dragons are bad."

Chapter 13: The Call of the Sea

Gathered in the library next week, Mark explained he had decided to write a poem about the sea. The children looked surprised and not entirely impressed, but he promised it would be short.

I dabbled in waves that softened the sun-baked sand
And dreamed of light and glistening seas, of charts and far-off lands.
Creating tales, that beckoned me, to step with firm-set heart
On to the deck, on to the deck, to journey deep and far.

And then there came a still calm voice, that caused me to pause, and to hold.
"Welcome, fair child, tread carefully now, be cautious as well as be bold.
The sea has mixed faces, it has its strange moods, it will charm and terrify you.
Sorrows and joys will come with the waves which break on the old and the new."

"I am ready," I cried. "The journey begins, the wind may drive where it wills.
Monsters and storms will not change my course, I fear nothing of good or of ill."
Stern and solemn now seemed the strange voice, as it said, as quiet as the deep,
"Only a fool is never afraid of the wildness and breadth of the sea."

I dreamed I stood still, then turned to go back, my heart now close to despair.
"Will I never be able to set sail ahead, to see the wide everywhere?"

"I did not say that. I did not say that. You may sail to the world's end.
But, be wary in face of the changing winds. Be humble, whatever they send."

I dabbled in waves that softened the sun-baked sand
And dreamed of light and glistening seas, of charts and far-off lands.
But now the dream is stronger, the calm voice will guide me through
When the time is right, when the time is right, I will board the deck anew.

Sarah looked at Mark. She opened her mouth as if about to speak, and then said nothing.

Thoughtfully, laboriously, Jason repeated. *"I did not say that, I did not say that."* and then continued: "But when the voice was saying that, it was inviting the person to think about what was actually said, and what was not said. It was not saying they should not travel."

"We are to travel," said Mark. "With our eyes wide open."

Chapter 14: The Battle Becomes Clearer

Mark looked around the group. "Well, that is it for today, I think next week is our last time, and then it is the holidays."

Jason put up his hand. "Mr Lind, I have a question. How did Prior John know that the Grail was not in the forest?"

"You have a good memory to take us back to the first chapter," said Mark. "I shall have to think about that! Time to go now, everyone."

Trudy, Sarah and Jason began to go to the exit, as did Mr Cook. Miss Smith stayed where she was. When the others had left she said: "Thank you for all your stories. I am glad Jason asked his question, I was wondering that, too."

"I will think about that, I really will. It is an interesting question."

Miss Smith did not move. "We would be very grateful. And I have been wondering if we could reward you for all your efforts. I shall have a word with our Head Teacher, Mrs Hutchinson. I realise I have not even told her your name." And then she got up and joined the others.

Mark walked as usual towards the folly, but the gate to the garden area of the park was padlocked. He turned aside and sat on a bench and thought about the afternoon. *Two people focusing on the Grail, the way through to the folly blocked. Does this mean anything?*

Someone else sat down on the other end of the bench. It was a warm day but they were well-wrapped, as if against winter snows, and Mark could not make out the features, and could not immediately tell whether it was a man or woman.

"Mr Lind," the person spoke, and it was a woman's voice. "I commend to you the questions this afternoon. In your interests, perhaps very much in your interests, and indeed to prevent harm to you, find out why Prior John was so certain."

"Who are you?" asked Mark. He had not recognised the voice. He looked sideways and was about to say more, but the person got up, and, with a slight nod of the head, walked off. Mark decided not to follow.

And then someone else was running to the bench. It was Jane, and Mark stood up.

"The meeting place is changed," she said breathlessly. "They must have known about us and someone closed the garden area and the folly down for today. Come with me."

They walked quickly across the park, out onto a different road, across and into a coffee-shop on the other side. Jane led Mark towards the back and he could see that five familiar people were sitting at a table in the corner. He was about to join them when he heard the café door open behind him; he glanced round and Agnes was hurrying in.

"I am so glad I have found you," she said. "Miss Smith came back after you left and..."

Mark held up his hand. "Come and join us, I think your story is better told here."

The three approached the table, and Agnes shrank back slightly. She knew Rex English, Jenny Loss, Emma and Gary Ladd, but the fifth, powerfully built and sitting straight, she did not know. And somehow the five together created a feeling she could not quite name.

Rex English stood. "Welcome kind messenger Jane, welcome the storyteller, welcome gentle Agnes. I think we can fit round the table if we sit close. "

Chairs were borrowed from neighbouring tables, spaces were made.

Agnes looked across at the person she did not know.

"My name is Mr Vincent," he said. "And I am guessing you are Agnes, a person I understand to be of truth and courage." He stood up. "I greet you."

Agnes gulped slightly and said nothing.

Mr English spoke: "We are gathered because the Le Fay search for the Grail continues, and Agnes, you are welcome to our counsels, and I know you will not repeat elsewhere what you might hear." He smiled at her, and then continued: "Interest was aroused when Prior John, in Mark's story, made it clear he knew something of what had happened to the Grail. The Le Fays, brother and sister, wonder whether he knew exactly what happened to it, where in Glastonbury it lies."

"I thought it was just a story," said Agnes.

"We learnt long ago that there is no such thing as *just a story*," said Jane, with a slightly staged sigh, and she smiled across the table.

"Agnes, you are right to make that point," said Jenny. "Because that troubles the Le Fays, too. Does Mark know more than he is letting on, and carelessly or deliberately allows Prior John to reveal more than he should? Or does he know no more than anyone else?"

"In the story, Prior John said very little."

"But when you are desperate, you will clutch on to any straw. And the Le Fays are desperate."

"Why?" asked Agnes.

"It consumes their thoughts," said Mr English. "They have become addicted to the idea of destroying it. They hate being thwarted, and they have been thwarted. They will not rest easy until it is gone. Their reasons used to be clear, the Grail stands for all that is good, for liberation and love, justice and sacrifice, nourishment and new beginnings. They want to crush it because it may yet disturb the mindset held (perhaps unknowingly) by such as Mr Edge, or, before him, more intentionally, by Mr Moore. It gets in the way of their plans to control what people think, but now the reasons seem increasingly mixed up with their visceral hatred of the Grail in itself. They will not let go. They hate for the sake of feeding the hate."

"Is the Grail in any danger?"

"I do not think they can find it," said Gary Ladd. "I do not think they can hear its clear call. They do not want it as it is." As before, he spoke in a slow and golden voice, but there was a lightness to it. It was more Spring than Autumn.

Jenny said, "Mark, we fear that you are the one who is in danger. They will want to know how much you know."

"What can they do to me?" asked Mark.

"We live in a physical world," said Mr Vincent. "And people sometimes use physical means. If they choose to use them, I am here to protect you."

"Or they will threaten you with some sort of lie, making something up, smearing your name. Perhaps an unjust accusation. Or a minor mistake made into something much larger," said Mr English.

"That is more likely," agreed Mr Vincent. "They don't like getting their nice suits dirty." He chuckled. And Agnes felt that he was probably nice, but just a little scary.

"What do I do?" said Mark.

"Two things," said Mark English. "Tell another chapter of the story next week, before it finishes for the holidays. Try and dampen down any reference to the Grail. Mr Vincent will be somewhere close at hand if anything happens once the children have gone."

"And the second?"

"We need to find a way of you telling stories to each of the children and to Mr Cook. I do not know their needs, not what the stories should be, but they are there in the library for a reason, and you may be able to help."

"Why not Miss Smith?"

"There may come a time for that."

Chapter 15: Playing the Game Well

"I shall help," said Emma. She and Mark were walking away from the café. "Old and young Merlins as we are. Tell me what you know about the children."

Mark did not know very much at all, and could only repeat, as far as he could remember, the reactions of Trudy, Jason, and Sarah, as the story had unfolded. Emma said, "I don't think we know enough to choose which person has which story. You could replace whatever you were going to do with your children in the forest with an end of term 'special'."

Mark nodded. "That sounds wise. Arthur has more faith in me than I do," he said with a smile. "I would be concentrating too much on worrying if I had the right story for the right person, and forget the story itself. This feels safer, and who knows whether different parts of different stories might help different people?"

They turned back into the park, found a bench, and began to plan.

In the library next Monday, Mark began…

***

When Edward and Agnes arrived back at the monastery Prior John was waiting for them.

"Thank you for taking food to Cuthbert," he said, gravely.

"May I ask a question?" said Edward. "When we first talked about the Grailstand, you said the Grail itself was no longer here, that it had gone a long way away. How did you know that?"

"That is the tradition. It is to be found in the west, but that no one knows exactly where. I am sure it is not here, it would have been found by now, or whispers would have turned to searching, by others apart from dragons."

***

Jason looked disappointed. Miss Smith sat forward and pursed her lips thoughtfully. *Does she believe me?* wondered Mark. *Have I said enough?* And then, with a slight shiver: *Who was the person who spoke to me on the bench?*

Jason said, in a voice that sounded as if he was trying hard still to sound friendly. "I thought the Prior was sounding more certain than your explanation. I would have thought there is a better story there, can't you think of one?"

"Sometimes we only catch glimpses. Our imaginations need to fill the gaps. Perhaps you could write another story about that, your own version?"

Jason smiled. "I will have a go."

Miss Smith sat back, her face was expressionless.

Mark decided he needed to move on. "Because it is our last gathering before the holidays, we are going to do something different. I will tell four different stories, and you can make of them what you will."

"Why four?" Miss Smith interrupted. "If you had five you could have one for each of us? I am sure none of us would like to feel we are left out."

"Thank you, Miss Smith, I think we only have time for four, and we can all share them."

"It would be fun to have a story each!" said Sarah, "Please, Mr Lind."

Mark smiled and held up his hand in surrender. "I will see if I can think of a fifth. But I do not know which story is for which of you, or perhaps all of them are for all of us. You can choose as is right for you, and perhaps your choice today would be different from your choice tomorrow, so let's hear them all, and they can rest with you. I need to be honest, the five are not really stories, just observations.

"Many years ago I told two stories about a boy called Tommy, this next one is about him."

***

Tommy was older now. There were many days when life seemed good, and some which felt not so good, when things did not go quite his way, when he was not sure he was handling situations well, when things just seemed confusing. He walked through the village, passed the old shop where the candle-maker had used to work, and on to where a friend of his mother lived. He took an interest in Tommy, was always there for him, never intrusive but wanting to be wise and helpful if needed. Often they talked about nothing of apparent importance but sometimes there would be something on Tommy's mind, and they would talk it through together. One afternoon Tommy was sitting there, quite quiet, and Elbek (an unusual name, but that is what it was) said, "Say what you are thinking."

"If this is a game, I don't always know the rules," said Tommy, ruefully.

"Is what a game?"

"Living." He said it blandly, not dramatically, but there was a slight smile there as well, because he knew it sound like a cliché.

Elbek did not quite smile, but there was a sparkle in his eyes. He replied, "I think that is an interesting metaphor, a helpful one." He reached for his cup of tea, realised it was empty, and put it back on the table.

He closed his eyes. "The attraction of the idea of *game* as a picture of living has been rightly popular. Perhaps this is because game and sport express many complex desires, all part of our humanity." He opened his eyes and said sharply: "I think you have used a good image."

Tommy knew Elbek well enough to know that sometimes he moved to another level. He loved that, and was keen not to distract, whilst knowing that he might need to encourage. He did not want him to stop talking.

"Does it depend on the type of game?" Tommy asked. And he noticed the old man's eyes flicker and knew he had kept the ball rolling.

"Let me think of some examples of games it could be like," said Elbek. Tommy sat back, and waited.

"It could be like a jigsaw puzzle. There we have the steady process of turning the pieces face up so we know with what we are dealing, the importance of putting the borders in place, the satisfaction of seeing the picture develop. There we are reminded that to force the wrong piece in the wrong place does not end well, that patience and gentleness are key qualities in playing this game. We have the valuing of every piece – every different part of your life matters, Tommy, and every person matters. And you matter just as much as anyone else. In a jigsaw the pieces are different, individual;

think how boring it would be if each piece was exactly the same. And with a jigsaw, we know that we will win, the picture will be completed, however long it takes. And with each new piece in the right place, it all becomes slightly easier.

"Or life could be like playing a game of chess. Where we need to try and think through the consequences of our actions, of our moves. Where we need to be aware of our weak areas, our weak positions. What does it profit if we make a dramatic attack on the right only to leave our Queen and Knights hopelessly exposed on the left? It is a game of patience and concentration, and of empathy, we need to learn how the mind of our opponent works. We need to remember the value of our pawns, that one or two in the right places can blunt an attack and lead to victory.

"Or, not quite a game, but imagine you are going for a walk along a cliff, but you have vertigo, heights trouble you. You are scared of losing your balance and are terrified of falling. But you have to stay on the path, it is the only way forward. You may choose to drop to your hands and knees, undignified, but it works, so you will do it. Or you can find a friend to walk between you and the edge; it will need to be a friend who is sure of foot and whose arm or hand is firm. You find a way of keeping going forward, however frozen with terror you may feel yourself to be.

"Or batting in a cricket match. You will be mindful of the weather, of the times when you need to score fast or slow. You will be mindful of the batsman at the other end: can you communicate well? Can you run equally quickly? Each bowler will have a different approach, but they want to get you out, and the pitch may be uncertain. How well you defend is as important as how well you attack. The longer you can stay in, the more runs you will score. But when you are out, when your wicket is fallen, then a rueful smile and getting ready for the next game. Who stops playing cricket because one innings goes wrong? And you are to play with a noble and honourable heart. That is as important, more important, than numbers on the board.

"And finally, a treasure hunt. There are clues to be found and questions to be answered. It is important to do them one at a time, in order, and not to leap ahead, because the final finding might depend on all the clues coming together. But imagine that, just to confuse us, there are lots of different treasure trails, but not all lead to the treasure that we really want and need. For you to reach the treasure that matters, you need to stay true to the original quest, the first guidance, and not be tempted by enticing other trails that cross your path. And so you need to know what treasure you really want, and why."

Elbek stopped. They both sat quietly. Elbek reached again for his cup and again stared at it, as if surprised by its continued emptiness.

Tommy said, "I am juggling all sorts of pictures in my mind! At different times I must be playing different games."

"You speak well. We all play different games. And these images are only glimpses."

Tommy shrugged. "It is all a bit much."

"Yes," said Elbek, "Life is, and so we do what we can. And, Tommy, remember the candle-maker. And how much what she did, meant to you."

"I am unlikely to forget," said Tommy.

"Ah, people do, people do. They become busy and distracted, and the important memories can fade too much from sight." Elbek smiled. "But with the right nudging they can usually be brought back." And he looked at Tommy and said, "Please remember, you are much loved, and you matter."

***

Mark looked round the little group in the library. He decided to let the silence stay. No one was quite looking at him in the eye, and everyone seemed lost in their own thoughts. Eventually he stood up.

"It is time to end now, thank you for your attention in these weeks. I hope you have a good summer holiday. I don't know if we are continuing next term, I expect someone will tell us when we need to know." He suddenly realised this all sounded rather blunt.

"Who was the candle-maker?" asked Sarah.

"That was another story," said Mark. "Perhaps one day I will tell it again." He walked towards the exit. There he stopped and said to Agnes, "I expect we will see each other again, that seems to be the pattern with those caught up in Arthur's world."

Agnes looked startled, and then said: "I hope so. I will miss you on these Mondays. Look, the children have caught up with you."

Mark turned. "Thank you," said Trudy, "for telling us the stories. I hope we can have some more." Sarah and Jason nodded.

"You have been kind listeners," said Mark. "I hope so, too. But remember, if it is not me or this library, you can always hear stories in many other places. Just make sure they are good ones to hear."

Sarah said: "You finished in a hurry. I really like your stories. And you just stopped."

Mark looked at her. "I am sorry. I am not very good at this."

Their eyes met and there was a flash of mutual understanding. "I'll think it through," said Sarah, gently.

There was a pause and then Mr Cook and Miss Smith came forward and briefly thanked Mark. Miss Smith then said, "May I walk to the park with you? That is your usual way home, I think."

"Of course," said Mark.

Chapter 16: Violence and Rescue

They walked in silence until they reached the park. Miss Smith then stopped and said, "The last game, the treasure hunt, that was aimed at me, wasn't it."

"When you asked for a fifth, I had to think of one quickly. But it was there for everyone, as the others were."

"You are right, Mr Lind, about our deciding which treasures we seek. The treasure you seek is different to mine. I will not be thwarted." A cold thrill went through Mark: the voice had changed, it was now that of the woman on the bench. She smiled that Mark had noticed. "Yes, there is one of me, but I have different voices and different disguises. My name is Morgan Le Fay."

Mark said, trying to be calm, "I should have guessed, and I know enough of your story to know that you were not always what you have become. I wonder what treasure-trail distracted you? Where did you begin to lose your way?"

Le Fay said: "This is your last walk in the park, your last walk, anywhere. And so it will not matter to tell you. I know you are scared so stop pretending to be brave. I, on the other hand, am bold and unashamed, and completely in control. It is power, the satisfaction of being able to shape the lives of others, to manipulate or bend them to my will. And of course what I do will ultimately be right for them, as they become subsumed into my world. I do it for their sake as well as mine."

Mark realised his voice unexpectedly sounded tired (*what effect does she have?*) but strangely felt less scared, and replied: "I guessed that. About the power I mean, not about how many times you think I will walk in the park. And I disagree that you are doing it for their sake, you are deceiving yourself." He paused and asked, almost conversationally, "What is your current strategy? Or may I guess?"

"One last little Merlin moment? One last attempt to play at levels well above you?"

Mark said slowly, "I think that your aim is always to cause hate and mistrust. I look around and wonder if your current strategy is to encourage people to think that words can mean whatever they want them to mean, and that their chosen meaning is the only right one. But they do not extend that right to others. If someone chooses a different meaning, then that can used as an excuse to hate them, to despise them, to bring them down. It means that nothing will be special, nothing will be valued, nothing can be protected. It will cause chaos. People will be terrified of using a word in the wrong way. How they used it in the past is now unacceptable.

"The only authority will be the strength of people's feelings, the weight they give to their own experience, and their ability to spread their views quickly. Their feelings, their determining of the meaning of a word, are all that counts. The teaching of the past, the shared understanding of the generations, becomes as nothing. I wonder if in the long-term you aim for the time when people will not dare label themselves as human, less that word is deemed offensive. They will be encouraged to see themselves as merely a living thing, no more important than a rat or, later, no more important than a sack of potatoes, and will thus have no sense of their intrinsic value, and will be ashamed even to have a desire to have such a sense. Thus you shall destroy their spirits, they will become as slaves to you.

"Anything that causes hate and fear, confusion and despair, is on your side. If you can reach the point when people will hate each other, will fight each other, because they cannot agree on the meaning of a word, then your work is nearly done. Even better if you can reach the stage where people will take violent offence against an unintended, unnamed, perceived implication behind the use of a word. People will stop talking to each other. They won't dare to speak, and it won't be too long before they will not dare to think.

"And you will be the strong ones, you will be the ones setting the agenda, changing the use of words as you wish to cause chaos. And then you will step in, and determine everything, and dominate. My guess is that this is your plan?"

Miss Smith kept her eyes fixed on the path ahead. She was walking quite quickly now, as if time was on her mind. "A pretty speech," she eventually said. "Have you been practising? You know that no one listens to you. Perhaps you rehearsed it in front of a mirror."

"Be cautious. You will end up controlling nothing that is worth controlling," said Mark. "Your satisfaction will be empty."

"Whether your guess is right or wrong, you won't be here to see it," she said dismissively, and beckoned to some figures on a bench they had now almost reached. The two men got up and came towards them. "Take Mr Lind, you know what to do. And to make sure he is nice and quiet…" She took something out of her pocket and jabbed it sharply into Mark's side. He slumped, and the two men held him roughly between them. "Not too much," she whispered fiercely. "I want your mind to be awake enough to see the irony of all your little heroics, all your dreams of being part of your little circle (where are they now, by the way? Isn't it strange they never help when really needed) coming to an end, and you coming to an end, by something as mundane as falling down a dirty railway cutting. I want you to know the sadness of despair. No more little stories or bad poems. Mr Lind. It's over."

She stepped back. The two men, half-holding, half-dragging Mark, began to walk towards the railway that went through trees outside the edge of the park. They were only a few yards away. Mark knew what would happen, but was too weak to struggle, and his mouth seemed paralysed. Miss Smith watched them for a moment, and then turned and walked away.

Where is Lancelot? Surely this is not how it is meant to end? Why does Le Fay hate so much? And even in his drugged and desperate state he caught himself internally discussing questions: *Because fear and hate reach a point where they are no longer rational. I wonder when that happened to her.* But by now they reached the railings. The two men without hesitation lifted Mark up and threw him over. They then vaulted over themselves. It all happened in seconds. *Someone will have noticed? But the park was nearly empty when I arrived, perhaps now there is no one around.* And Mark had landed heavily and his consciousness was slipping, his mind was now fading. *Perhaps she injected stronger than she thought.* He could not lift up his head to look around. He felt himself being lifted and dragged again. The top of the cutting to the railway line was very close.

The attack was sudden. All Mark felt was the grip on each arm torn away. He collapsed, and as he fell he heard two crashes. There was silence, then someone leaned down and passed something under his nose, which woke him with a splutter. The someone then poured a few drops of something into his mouth.

Gary Ladd stood up, it was he who had been ministering to Mark. Mr Vincent was standing next to him. Mark sat up and looked around. One of his assailants was lying in front of a tree, the second in front of another.

"We did not actually hit them," explained Mr Vincent. "Sometimes to be swung hard against a tree has the same effect. They are stunned, nothing more, and will have sore heads, and some explaining to do. But they did not see us and so do not know what happened; that will embarrass them. That may mean they will not report this for a little while, but when they do, the Le Fays will guess."

Mark slowly sat up, still very drowsy, still finding it difficult to speak. After a moment he whispered: "It is easy to forget how strong you are."

Mr Vincent smiled. "It is an old temptation. Try to resist it."

Chapter 17: Glimpses of the View

Sitting round the table in the café were Jane, Mr English, Jenny, Agnes, and Emma. Mark, still dazed, sat between Jane and Emma.

"What do we do now?" asked Jane. "Given what they tried to do to Mark, this feels really serious."

"It has always been serious," said Mr English. "They dislike the good stories and they have become obsessed with the Grail. They are increasingly frightened that they may not win. They are desperate."

"Shouldn't we tell the police?" asked Agnes. "I certainly don't want that Miss Smith back in my library."

Mr English smiled. "You are right to be practical and right not to want her there. We have told the police, and they will do what they can. The two men are being sought, my guess is that Miss Smith has already disappeared."

"Are you not worried they will do it again? Try to get rid of Mark?" Agnes said.

"They have always been trying to get rid of Mark, or at least what he represents and what he brings to the table; they have simply changed their methods. But they know, or will have guessed, that the protection has increased. Lancelot and Galahad are not to be discounted lightly. I could get several testimonials from giants, dragons and knights to that effect. No, we need not be scared, and it would not help us if we were. But, as always, we should be thoughtful and watchful. It is not always a friendly world."

Agnes nodded, turning many things over in her mind.

"Let us honour Mark," said Jenny Loss, "it can be difficult to be Merlin, it can be costly to tell good stories. Mark, you have been kept safe, and we are grateful."

There was a pause, quite a long one, and then Agnes said: "May we hear a story now? I feel I need one. Something about hope."

Emma and Mark looked at each other. Mark was still not looking quite himself. Emma smiled and said: "I think I'll do this one."

***

Tracey was not completely looking forward to the school trip, The decisions about what clothes to wear, who else would be on the coach, whom she would sit next to, other pupils' behaviour in a different place, all meant that that she slept badly the night before. But it was different, a change, and there was a small part of her that felt excited and adventurous.

But only a part. And the journey was disappointing, her best friend had found another best friend, and Tracey had sat next to Louise, which was fine but not great. And then the teachers explained that the walk was quite long, and that the lunch might be late.

They trudged off, and then trudged on. On the left was the side of a steep hill, on the right a high thick hedge. Occasionally Tracey could peer through small gaps in the branches and catch glimpses of a wild and beautiful landscape, mountains and forests, waterfalls and shining grass. But a step forward and the view was lost again, and might not be seen again for a hundred more steps.

Eventually, eventually, they reached the hall where lunch would be served.

The host greeted them, and asked: "Did you enjoy the walk?"

No one replied. They were not nervous of him, but they were of each other. And then he looked directly at Tracey. "How about you, did you enjoy the walk?"

Tracey breathed deeply. And said, "Yes, but I was not sure why the hedge was so thick and high. We seemed to be missing a wonderful view? Occasionally there were tiny gaps and I saw something, but very little. We have come all this way and it seemed frustrating." She had not meant to end up sounding cross or upset, but somehow it now felt safe to say what she felt.

The host bowed slightly. "You have answered well. And you ask a good and important question. The owner decided that if anyone caught sight of the view for too long, they would be so transfixed that they would never continue the journey. It is a wonderful, fabulous, view. Such a sight needs to be hidden until the time is right; we may be given glimpses but they need to be brief and narrow, not enough fully to distract.

"And now the time is right, the journey is done; come with me, all of you, and we will look at the view, from the hilltop, all around, in all its glory."

And he led them to the hall, and there they saw that one side was open, and, looking through and out, they gazed in wonder at a view beyond all their imaginings.

***

After a time, Agnes said "Thank you." And then: "Oh, with everything else I forgot. Mr Cook left an envelope in the library as he was leaving. It is for you." She drew the envelope out of her coat pocket and handed it to Mark.

Chapter 18: Return to St George's

Dear Mark

You may not remember me. I was a pupil at St George's, became involved with Mr English/Arthur and met you once or twice. I have heard that it is you who has been telling stories to three of our children in the library. Thank you for all you have done this term.

Would you like to come in and say hello? It would be good to see you again. Are you still in touch with any of the others? If you are, please tell Emma that I remember her.

Yours sincerely

Annabel Hutchinson, Headmistress, St. George's.
P.S. I am married, hence the different surname!
P.P.S. I have given this letter to Mr Cook to give to you, and I am grateful to him for this.

Mark had read it to himself. He now read it aloud to the circle.

"Did you know?" He asked Mr English.

"No, or not quite," was the reply. "I have not had contact with Annabel and have not had contact with St George's. But I felt that there was a slight change in the air, I wondered if there was a new chapter. This is interesting and it feels positive that she wants to meet. I think you should go, and if Emma is free, she should go too."

"Might Miss Smith be somewhere there?" said Jane. "Might this be a trap? How do we know Annabel is still on our side?"

"We do not know," said Mr English. "But perhaps that is true of all attempts to reconnect. *Is the person still a friend?* That is always the question. I think the reference to Emma makes it seem less likely it is a trap, unless Annabel is being devious indeed. As to Miss Smith, there is no reason why she should be there in the holidays. And remember, the police are looking for her. She will want to be far away, there has been no sign of her anywhere. Always bear in mind that Miss Smith was a disguise, my guess is that the character no longer exists."

"And my guess is that Sir Richard is prepared to ride out once again, yet again," said Mark with a smile. "I'll write."

Annabel's response was swift, and two weeks later Emma and Mark were sitting in her study at St George's. The greetings had been warm, and any lingering worry had disappeared from Mark's mind.

"Why did you write?" he asked.

"There was something special about those days," answered Annabel. "The stories, the conversations, room 868. This seemed an opportunity to bring them back to mind. Emma, your stories were particularly important for me, so I wondered if I could reach you through Mr Lind, or Mark as I should call him now. When it all happened back in those days I felt I was being introduced to a much bigger, somehow, strangely, a much more *real* world. But the years went by, and the memories faded, and then I heard that someone called Mr Lind was in the area, telling stories to my pupils." She paused. "Are the others close-by as well?"

Emma said, "They are. And thank you for remembering the stories."

"Well, I don't remember all the details, but I remember how they made me feel. And that was important." A slightly more business-like, Headmistress-tone became apparent, still warm, but the voice of a leader with a purpose in mind. Emma smiled to herself, remembering the child of many years before. Annabel continued: "I would like some of that feeling back in my school. Emma, would you consider working here?"

Emma smiled. "Me?" She looked over at Mark. "You've got the real one there."

Annabel said politely, "I am sure Mark is very good, and the children in the library have enjoyed their times there. It is just that I have not heard him as much as I used to listen to you."

Emma said, "If Mark is content, I am happy to say yes. He would say that I do not need his permission, but I respect him too much to take his place if that would be wrong. Dare I say, he is not a young man. This could be his last hurrah!"

"Time moves on," Mark smiled. "Emma, you are very kind. I would be very pleased to know that you are here, and then in due time the role will pass to someone else. It was never really 'my' place. I occupied it for a time, and now it will be you. The important thing is that the role is provided and protected; as it was by Mr English, as it is now by Annabel."

"It need not be a completer either/or," said Annabel. "Mark, I think I would like you still to be around, too, somewhere in the background, if that were possible, as a friend of the school?"

"I would be honoured and pleased to be a friend of the school once again."

"That's very good," said Annabel. "And now I am expecting some visitors. Please stay, I think you might be glad to see them." She went to the door, beckoned, and Trudy, Sarah, and Jason came in. They stood there, nervously: in the Headmistress' study, in school in the holidays, the man from the library there, a lady they did not know; it all felt quite strange.

"Let's everybody sit," Annabel said. "All of us," and made introductions between the children and Emma.

"Mr Lind," she continued. "What happened in the library was valuable, and we thank you. Would you be happy to carry on next term? And some more pupils may join."

"Certainly," said Mark. "And will Mr Cook and Miss Smith be accompanying them?"

"We shall arrange suitable support indeed." And Mark sensed he was not to ask more. Instead he said, "Trudy, Sarah, and Jason. If I am to continue, it would help me to know if there is anything I should do differently?"

"I thought the stories were good, but your characters are all quite trusting," said Trudy. "I think more caution would be more realistic."

Jason said: "I liked the stories, especially the dragon, but sometimes it all seemed a bit slow, like the Hermit section. And I still think the dragon-companion should have been punished."

"I liked it, and I think you kept trying to do your best," said Sarah.

Mark's eyes flickered, and he looked long at the table, another moment when time seemed to be standing still. He pondered for a while what to say: "Thank you for that and thank you all of you. More next term, then."

"May we have something now, very quick, if Mrs Hutchinson does not mind. What happened to Edward and Agnes when they grew up?" This was Trudy, and she glanced at her Headmistress, who nodded.

"Well," said Mark, "a good question." He thought for a while, and then said, "Agnes became an Abbess, looking after a community in a monastery, and became known for her great learning and wisdom. Edward became a Brother in his monastery; as the years went by Brother James and Prior John became ill and died, and there was another Prior. Brother Edward, as he had become, was content to read and study, to write and teach. His mother became frail, and so she moved into the monastery grounds, into a small room against the outer wall. Edward kept the Grailstand, and whenever he needed help to forgive someone (or if he himself needed forgiving) he would look at it and remember the dragon-companion. Agnes and Edward saw each other often."

"Learning and forgiveness," said Annabel, nodding. "Good themes."

"And we can add an adjective," said Mark. "*Rigorous* learning and *rigorous* forgiveness. Members of the communities would often note that Edward and Agnes were friendly but clear-eyed. And the very sharp-eared would hear them, when chatting together, sometimes mutter words like *Lancelo*t or *Cuthbert* or *Etheldreda.*" The children smiled.

Annabel looked slightly askance (she had become rather used to having the last word), but then relaxed. "Thank you,

Mr Lind; with you and Emma here, we will build something strong."

The group chatted for a little longer and the three pupils left.

"Miss Smith?" asked Emma.

"I have not seen her since the Monday before the end of term," said Annabel. "That is why I was hesitant about promising anything about her presence next term."

"The Le Fays have a particular interest in St George's because of Gary being here and the link to the Grail all those years ago. They cannot let go," said Mark. "And Miss Smith is a Le Fay. But I do not think you will see her for some time."

Annabel looked away, and then out of the window, her mind turning over memories of confrontation in the corridor, of a candle burning in room 868.

"I am feeling, I am feeling… how can I put this? Re-awakened, that's the word. Re-awakened. And protected. And, if I may say, determined. Emma, Mark, you will be welcome here as much as you are able. Will I see the others?"

"They are close at hand. You are indeed protected this morning. We were not completely sure how things might be, there are one or two quietly guarding the school in case we were interrupted. May I?" Mark walked to the window and waved.

Annabel came and stood by him, and saw four or five, no, six or seven, figures walking towards the school. She shivered slightly, but it was a happy shiver, a reminder of seeing figures in Glastonbury walking in the evening light.

"We can wait here for them," said Mark.

There was part of Annabel that suddenly wanted to be terribly practical and say: *"We don't have enough chairs."* But she did not, and just kept looking.

Rex English came in first, he bowed slightly to Annabel, then turned and whispered something to those behind him. They nodded and stepped back, and then hurried off. He smiled again at Annabel.

"Well done. And remember, whenever the candle is to be lit, I will not be far away." He stood still for a few moments, Annabel felt somewhat overwhelmed and stood, waiting. Mr English then said, "Ah, here it is, I wondered if it might be useful for you to have this back. And some chairs."

Mr Vincent and Gary Ladd rolled the table sideways to get it through the door. Behind them Annabel saw Jenny Loss and Jane. With them were two people she did not recognise, and then Mr Cook, and then an old man who seemed vaguely familiar. Mr Cook and Jane were carrying chairs. There was a slight struggle as the other table was taken out of the room, but then all was settled.

Annabel suddenly recognised the old man. "Mr Aldwyn!" she said.

"Once an old friend, always an old friend," said Mr Aldwyn, in a more quavering voice than Annabel remembered.

She held out her hands and he took both in his. "You gave Emma space to tell the stories," She said. "I will always be grateful." She looked around. "It is so good to see other old friends again. I cannot quite believe it. And who…?"

"This is Izzy," said Mr English, "who, with Jane, helped Mark tell stories many years ago, and this is Agnes who has recently done the same. Now, I think the table is ready and we have enough chairs. Let us sit."

He looked across at Annabel. "You are the Headmistress; we wait on you. Thank you for having us here."

Annabel smiled round the room. "I am not sure I had much choice. But perhaps I did, I think I remember enough of these encounters to know that if, somewhere deep within, I had not wanted this, then it may not have happened. Thank you all for being here, it is an honour for me, and, as I said to Mark and Emma, a moment of re-awakening."

She looked at Mr English. "Why are you here, now?"

"We wish to offer support, and protection. And we enjoy seeing each other once again, and to be reminded of the breadth of the table. And indeed, if I may put it like this, the *length* of the table; some of us have not seen each other for a long time but still feel part of the same story. One of us (here he smiled at Mr Cook) is very new to all this and wants to know more." He looked up, a question in his voice: "Perhaps also we should have let the children stay?"

Jane glanced out of the window. "They have not gone far," she said cheerfully. "They are staring at us from the car park, no doubt wondering about these strange people who have suddenly appeared."

"Shall we call them in?" Asked Mr English and looked at Annabel: "It is your choice."

Annabel knew her pupils well, and her mind raced through the backgrounds. Life for none of them had been easy. Sometimes it had been dangerous and there was a fragility in their trust of others. They could be unpredictable. But they had agreed to the library idea and had listened to the stories. Perhaps she owed it to them to let them be part of things.

"I shall go and ask," she said, and left the room.

Those who remained stayed silent. It felt like a deep breath before the plunge into a lake. There was a slight and quick shuffling, as if people were flexing again muscles not recently used. *And so it begins* thought Mark.

As Annabel walked the children back towards the building, she explained that there were some unexpected guests, friends of Mr Lind, and that it seemed good to meet.

The children came in, nervously once again, what a strange day this was becoming. Extra chairs were fetched, and spaces were made round the table. There were more introductions and welcoming smiles. The children relaxed a little and, before anything else happened, Jason asked: "May we have a story about Tommy?"

Mark glanced at Annabel, saw the affirming nod, and began.

***

When Tommy left his old friend Elbek to walk back through the village, the road had become busier. People and carts crowded through. He noticed a father with a child close behind, walking slowly, carefully and resolutely to one side of the busy traffic, making solid progress. But in the noise and the busyness the child dropped a little further behind and Tommy wondered if the father was aware. The child nearly stumbled on a cobble, and a passing cart came perilously close. Neither the child nor the driver noticed the other, too busy concentrating on the road ahead. Tommy walked more quickly but then slowed down once he was closer behind the child. He did not quite know what to do: he was a little shy generally, and he did not want to startle her by suddenly speaking. He was not very large, so he undid the front of his jacket, pulled the two halves to the sides and made himself look twice as big. If a rider or driver came close, they would likely see him, whereas they might not have seen the child. He could have easily passed by the girl, and knew that his own mother might now be wondering why he was late home, but he kept to the necessary slow pace, a few steps behind, silently providing protection as best he could.

It was not long before the father reached a corner and looked behind before turning into another, much quieter, road. For a moment he was concerned, but then their eyes met and the child hurried to catch up. All was well. Neither noticed Tommy, who had quietly brought his hands back down to his sides and was now looking like anyone else, walking along the busy road.

***

The story ended and the room fell quiet. The three children had stopped shuffling while Mark was speaking and were now sitting very still. "I like people like Tommy," said Trudy, breaking the silence. "So do I", said Jason and Sarah, in chorus.

"So do I," said Rex English. And the room was quiet again.

There are echoes here, this could almost be room 868 again, thought Emma. Annabel was following her own train of thought: *But what that room was or is, what it means, is more than the room itself.* And she smiled to herself: *With or without a candle.*

Gary Ladd looked across at her, nodded, took a candle from his pocket, lit it, and gently placed it in the middle of the table.

In this series, also published by New Generation Publishing:

The King and the Storyteller

The Knights and the Table

Other works by the author, published by Highland Books:

At the Harbourside

Worthy of Trust

This I call to mind

Letters from Henry

The Well-tempered Gallery

And also the cucumbers

Milton Keynes UK
Ingram Content Group UK Ltd.
UKHW011832100624
443885UK00004B/135